# The Shattered Realms

Shane Kind

# DEDICATION

To my Family, who patiently put up with my constant ramblings.

# CONTENTS

# ACKNOWLEDGMENTS

To J.R. Tolkien who dared me to dream, and to Bernard Cornwall who inspired me to tell a tale of my own, and to my daughter Hannah, who showed me the way to go about it.

# 1

# Prologue

Our story begins with a young child, aged ten, a foundling left on the doorstep of the church shortly after his birth, who was educated by the church and who even at a young age was able to recite great sections of scripture from memory and who, when not being a scamp, was such a reward to be around.

By the age of ten he stood just a couple of inches short of five feet, his eyes were of a piercing hazel colour and his hair was mousy brown, nothing else unusual except for two small bumps one on either ear lobe that would be missed by those who didn't stare.

However, the peace this young boy had enjoyed for the last ten years was about to be shattered as an attack on his village that night by a warband of Orsk would result in the death of every male old enough to wield a weapon and any women who was beyond child baring years.

The Orsk, since magic was dissipating in the world, had lost much of their cohesiveness and rationale, they were a backward facing race brutal and barbaric who lived in caves during the day and roamed wide and far during the night, there only allies were the lesser race of goblins who were nothing more than two legged rats and who lived even deeper in the earth.

Once the surviving prisoners were deep underground in the catacombs of the Orsk, the women and female children were separated from the young males. Where those unfortunate women and children went, the ten-year-old boy, did not know. He and his male compatriots, of the same age, were put to work immediately fetching and carrying for their Orsk masters. One of the most important aspects of life now, apart from being taught warcraft, was the forging and making of weapons and armour for an army they should hope never to meet, unlike any armour these boys had ever seen worn by man, these were called plate armour and each piece had flexible joints were required that allowed the host to be completely covered, unlike the more common chainmail that left lower arms and legs exposed. Even the weapons were different, these were no sleek swords with sharp cutting edges, they were big heavy cumbersome swords with a thick blunt back edge and a serrated front edge. These weapons were made for large creatures to wield who had little or no need for swordsmanship. Orsk masters would collect the weapons and armour at the end of every day and take them deeper into the underground cave system. Every once in a while, the boys caught the whisper of just two words, that brought fear into their hearts, the stuff of nightmares which even made the Orsk shiver and make signs to their Gods, those words were, 'Black Guard'.

The ten-year-old was given a new name by his Orsk masters, one befitting his new life and status, they called him, 'Ro-Gan' which meant 'will go far' in their language. Every Human boy was given a new companion, a grey-skinned half-blood, and Ro-Gan was paired up with a creature called On-Gar. On-Gar was neither a human nor an Orsk, he was a mix, a half-blood in Rogan's reckoning, but a Half-breed to the Orsk masters. While the masters taught the boys armour smithing, it was On-Gar's duty to teach Ro-Gan the art of warcraft, at first only with wooden weapons and crude bits of leather armour.

There was a simple and basic regime each morning, to help the new recruits to settle in to their new lives, it began each day by the Half-bloods coming round and unchaining each boy in their care, one of the first things that all of the boys, Human and Half-bloods, needed to do, was to strip down to there under garments and then proceed to shave off any noticeable hair before having their entire bodies painted with a green dye. The dye was derived from plants, so it was not actually harmful to any of them. Once that ritual was complete, they all got dressed for the day in a basic woolen tunic usually a faded brown colour, and darker brown trousers with brown leather boots, then it was off to another chamber where they would be fed a broth made from scraps.

.

## 2 COMING OF AGE.

How does one glean hope when it matters not if your eyes are open or closed, and there is no natural or artificial light to give even a glimmer of hope? When one rolls on ones back to look up at the stars and to pray to the one true God and there is nothing, no stars and no answer to those prayers.

When the winter chill begins to bite and it is all that you can do to curl tightly into a ball to keep warm, even when every muscle and sinew cries out to stretch and be free, but what is freedom when your nights are spent in chains and your days in enforced servitude.

And yet, you take another breath, and the tepid dry atmosphere causes your throat to tighten and gasp for yet more of that same filthy smelling dry air, why does life cling to one's bones when there is no useful purpose for it to do so, because, maybe, just maybe, God has not abandoned you, and today shall be the day that you rise up and bath in his almighty glory and he will deliver those who seek to devour you, into your own hands, and the Lord God say's vengeance is mine,

"Wake up! Ro-Gan no time to have a lay in." the smell of burning oil now permeated into the nostrils, seeking to

2

drive the smell of Human waste away, and it is a welcome smell, that ushers in the start of a new day.

That morning On-Gar was awake first and he was the one who lit the torches in the cave and in the corridor outside, the same thing was being repeated all down the corridor, in fact in hundreds of corridors that ran the length and breathe of the kingdom under the mountains.

Ro-Gan would then take the overnight bucket to the sluice pit and tip it away before swapping it for a bucket full of fresh spring water from the stream that ran down one side of the central cavern and down the corridor and out on to the moors.

Every morning the boys woke to the same routine, strip and shave, and then paint themselves all over with a thick green dye, all the Human boys and all of the Half-Orsk boys. The dye took no more time to dry than it did to administer, once that was done, they would dress in brown woolen tunics and trousers and slip into their soft leather boots. Ro-Gan was a good student and enjoyed more freedom in the underground settlement than most, of course he was not trusted as much as any of the half-breeds and certainly not as much as any of his orc masters. However, he had come learn that the Orsk were a dying breed since magic, the thing that seemed to have bound them all together was dissipating from the earth.

Unbeknown to Ro-Gan was a place called 'the breeding pits,' chambers where Human females lived and who were habitually raped by the Orsk and whose babies would become the foundation for the future of the Orsk race and who were called by their Orsk masters, the half-breeds.

Ro-Gan was one of only a few boys who could both speak and write Ingolandic, the common Human language of the Shattered Kingdoms and as he taught is best friend On-Gar the half-breed how to read and write, he in turn taught Ro-Gan, Wiaznuri, or black speech, the language of the orcs. Ro-Gan also spoke the language of the Elves, but he was yet to actually meet one to converse with so that part of his education he kept to himself.

Most nights Ro-Gan would struggle to get straight off to sleep and his hours were broken with wild dreams of Elves and men, sometimes he would see the face of a women who he called mother but that face never had features it was always blurred, then on other occasions he would be practicing sword craft with a man who dressed in the finest armour,

One of the reasons that the boys were told to paint themselves with the green dye was to deter them from trying to escape when they were allowed outside to hunt for food or they were involved in a raid, but as raids were predominantly carried out at night under the cover of darkness Ro-Gan figured you couldn't actually tell what colour any bodies skin was, they were all just a filthy brownish as it was hard to keep that clean, but he followed orders, not because he wanted to, far from it, from the first evening he was captured and dragged here, down to this very day, Ro-Gan plotted his escape, and as he got to know all the other captive boys he figured he take them all with him too.

The boys were from all backgrounds and all within a couple of years of each other in age, Ro-Gan was fifteen as he had counted down the years of his captivity. The half-breeds were mostly older by a couple of years but that was not true in every case. Each Human captive was paired with a Half-breed and together they learned to fight, they ate, worked together, and they slept in the same cave dwelling, it was not an idea mix but Ro-Gan was a charismatic boy who was determined to pull everyone together while he plotted and planned their great escape. Sometimes he would talk about escape with the half-breeds as well and to his surprise none of them ever told the orcs of his plans.

Today though was not a normal day, a normal day would consist of the whole band of boys and half-breeds working hard at the settlements forges all morning making

4

swords, daggers, helmets, and plate armour and the like, which was taken away and never seen again, even the Orsk local to the settlement never used any of the equipment they made not even while in the outside world, it was the first of many a puzzle that Ro-Gan had no idea the answer. All of the settlements equipment in fact came from what they stole or won on raids. However, today was the day of the coming-of-age ceremony and there was great excitement throughout the settlement, even amoungst the Orsk.

Ro-Gan's thoughts were interrupted by the sudden appearance of the orc chief, Snag-Roth.

Snag-Roth was a likable type even for an Orsk, most of the other orcs were cruel by nature and most definitely aloof in character, Snag-Roth was easy going and only seemed to want a quiet life arranging the affairs of his charges. He stood a little over five feet in Hight which seemed to be an average height for the orcs that Ro-Gan had seen, His age was unknown but if the scars on his face and upper arms were anything to go by, he had certainly lived a full and exerting life, perhaps this was where old orc warriors ended their days babysitting young captives.

"Ro-Gan, On-Gar get dressed for the day and follow me, quickly!" barked Snag-Roth.

"Where do we go in such a hurry?" Ro-Gan inquired, knowing full well where they would be taken, On-Gar was very excited and looking forward to testing his metal, Ro-Gan was just as excited but was trying his hardest to be indifferent in front of others.

Snag-Roth spoke quietly to Ro-Gan, "You have been training now with us for five winters it is time to for you to prove you are a warrior, it is your coming-of-age ceremony, you too On-Gar!" he called as they hambled down the tunnel that connected their space with the main arena, a great cavernous space at the centre of the settlement.

Now all the human boys and their half-breed

companions are gathered. And it would seem not just from Ro-Gan's part of the settlement but from the other two area's as well. Thirty-six boys along with thirty-six half-breeds, each pair being matched up to fight another pair, each are then given weapons, exact replicas of the real thing, but made from bone, it might have been wood but for the fact that not a single tree grew within leagues of this place, if hit by anyone of these implements, they could brake bone or at the very least bruise the flesh heavily.

Above the arena was a wooden walk way that ran all around the circumference of the cave and it slowly started to fill up with other orcs, they were all very eager to see how their young charges would fair in combat. The mood was very upbeat and in Ro-Gan's five winters here he had never seen anything like it, many Orsk shouted for certain young ones who they had come to know personally and many bets began to change hands and much drink was being consumed.

Chief Snag-Roth shouted for silence as the noise was beginning to reach fever pitch.

"The rules of the competition are simple, put your opponent down by any means, if your companion goes down and is unable to continue, he will fight alone in the next round."

"After the first round is over you will be given five minutes to gather yourselves for the next round, the round of forty-eight."

"The third round will be contested by those twenty-four who come through the forty-eight, and will be given a ten-minute rest period."

"The fourth round will be contested by those winning twelve, and they will be given a full fifteen-minute rest period."

"The six couples who make it to the fifth round will enjoy a half-hour brake, when the fighting commences you will notice a new team will have been added, give a cheer now and again when Chief's Lug-Ran and Bal-Dok grace

the arena with their mighty show of strength and agility."
The upper balcony erupted with shouts and cheers while
those who were about to fight stayed silent.

"The last two standing who reach the final will then
fight each other; the winner will be declared the leader of
this new warband."

"Let the fight begin!" shouted another Orsk chief from
somewhere up on the wooden walkway.

The contestants had been paired-up they lined up
outside the arena and the first four names were called.

By the time it was Ro-Gan's turn eight fighters had
been eliminated one with a broken arm another with blood
pouring from a face wound. Ro-Gan took moved to the
other side of the arena and took his stand broadsword in
hand, On-Gar was at his left side, he had chosen a war-
axe. Their opponents looked tense, continually shifting
their weight from one foot to the other. The chief orc
clanged a small hammer on the side of the arena signaling
that the fight should begin.

Straight away one of the other two lurched forward
towards Ro-Gan with his weapon of choice, a long mace,
held high over his head. Ro-Gan weighted a moment
before crouching down, his weight on the ball of his right
foot and his left leg out stretched, as the fighter drew level
with his left foot, Ro-Gan swirled his body round
broadsword in hand in low slicing cut from his right to
left.

The other fighter was trying to bring his weapon down
on top of Ro-Gan head when the broadsword hit his left
cracking the bone clean in two, if it had been a proper
sword the opponent would have lost both legs such was
the force behind the swing.

On-Gar's opponent was suddenly caught in two minds,
that was a fast take down of his team mate, he too was
using a clubbed weapon, and attempting to drive it
downward from over his own head. On-Gar took
advantage of the indecision and ran sideways at him with

his war-axe firmly clenched in both hands as he swiped with force into the gut of his opponent.

Both competitors were down writhing in agony, the match was over.

Being early in the draw it gave Ro-Gan and On-Gar the ability to watch the others and make mental note of how they fought. It was about another hour before round two began and this time they had been drawn against an opponent who partner had been knocked out in the last round, so he faced them alone. This time On-Gar made the first move by stepping forward bowing to the single opponent before placing his war-axe on the floor just Infront of his feet. The opponent smiled before launching his attack, his blade thrust forward in a full-frontal attack, quick as a flash On-Gar curled his right foot around the shaft of the axe, flicked it into the air, twirled it three times and then threw it at the oncoming opponent hitting square on the forehead. The unfortunate attacker hit the ground face first and was knocked out completely. Two rounds left.

After the second round all those couples who were left were allowed a quick water brake and a few minutes to recover, there was not one of those surviving competitors who wasn't covered in bruises or welts from head to toe.

In this next fight the orc chief allowed the contestants to take their starting positions before he threw only two weapons into the arena, a broadsword and a short sword. As soon as the competitors heard the clang Ro-Gan's opponent threw himself to the centre ground right arm outstretched clutching for the longer sword.

Ro-Gan did a move similar to one of his earlier bouts, he crouched low but instead of placing his left leg out for balance this time he swept it around catching his opponent just has he had clasped his right hand around the broadsword.

The force of Ro-Gan's kick knocked the blade straight to the feet of On-Gar who picked it up and began twirling it around in his right hand while in sighting his opposite number to dare attack without a weapon. Ro-Gan was still swirling around low to the ground when he caught On-Gar's opponent with a hard kick to the back of his calf.

As the stunned opponent turned to look at Ro-Gan, On-Gar ran forward and cracked him on the side of the head with the blunted broadsword, once more knocking his opponent clean out.

The round of the last six began the two half-breed chiefs were added to the contest, fortunately they were not Ro-Gan and On-Gar's opponents.

Ro-Gan and On-Gar exchanged a few brief words before the clang of the chief's hammer rang out. Ro-Gan immediate grabbed On-Gars left arm which was raised up towards On-Gar face as he clenched both hands tightly around On-Gar fist he was lifted off his feet and his legs were carrying him in a circular motion around On-Gar and back towards his opponent.

As he moved forward unsure quite what was happening as this bout was without weapons, On-Gar heaved Ro-Gan forward, Ro-Gan clasped his legs around the half-breed's neck before dropping the rest of his body like a dead weight toward the floor.

The half-breed was propelled forward head first over Ro-Gan and into the floor where On-Gar gave him an almighty great kick in the solar plexus, one down one to go. This time it was On-Gar who took the lead by running around back of the Human opponent as Ro-Gan fained a frontal attack.

The Human ignored On-Gar fearing Ro-Gan as the better fighter, and so he girded his loins and stood with his fists raised. However, to his surprise Ro-Gan threw himself down at his feet just before On-Gar drop kicked him from behind. Ro-Gan quickly cupped his arm around the Humans head and tried to suffocate him.

The Human was very strong and grabbed hold of Ro-Gan's arm and slowly started to pull it away so that he could catch his breath. It was at this point that On-Gar improvised and seeing the very real danger that this opponent would soon be on his feet he kicked him with all his might right between the legs.

The Orsk whose number had been growing around the arena suddenly began whooping and cheering this had been the best entertainment they had seen in a long time.

The next round came and went just as the last one had and has fate would seem to be the master of ceremonies, Ro-Gan and On-Gar met Lug-Ran and Bal-Dok in the final. Both newcomers were already battle harden warriors and to make things worse they had only fought in a couple of the previous bouts so they were relatively fresh.

Ro-Gan spoke quickly with On-Gar telling him that these two fought more like orcs than humans or indeed the other half-breeds, so they would be all about front attack and brawn over brains, Ro-Gan and On-Gar needed to be smarter and faster, Ro-Gan intermated a fighting style that they had been training and practicing for weeks, it was supposed to be used in their escape attempt but it would equally work here Ro-Gan thought.

The contest went on for much longer than any of the orcs had envisaged including the two who were fighting and there constant insistence of running straight at Ro-Gan and On-Gar was beginning to tell on them as their strength ebbed away, Shields drooped on arms and weapons were not held as high for the sweeping cuts, again On-Gar grabbed hold of Ro-Gan's left for-arm and was lifted in the air high enough to kick Bal-Dok full in the face as he failed to raise his shield in time.

One down, one to go, Lu-Ran had learned nothing it seemed and his attack was straight forward yet again, and the outcome was just the same Ro-Gan side stepped and parried Lug-Ran's war-axe, and On-Gar got round the back of him and hit him in the lower back with a mighty blow to his lower back. Lug-Ran was beaten and he felt to his knees screaming a blood curdling noise that acknowledged his defeat.

The final saw Ro-Gan pitted against On-Gar for the right to be called War-Chief but On-Gar had no desire either to fight his friend nor did he want the responsibility of being a War-Chief.

Never the less the rules were the rules and the two had to fight each other without weapons. Ro-Gan soon started to feel On-Gar's strength sapping as they wrestled each other this way and that, and the next time they both fell to the ground arms and legs entangled Ro-Gan was able to gain purchase with his legs around On-Gar's neck while holding his left arm out and up causing On-Gar to immediately slap his right hand down on the floor in submission.

Fifteen-year-old Ro-Gan was cheered by all that were present including when he looked up some of the Orsk masters, but the result also began a feeling of hatred amoungst both the defeated and the other Orsk masters. The rules were the rules and Ro-Gan had won fairly and squarely, and so the newly appointed War-Chief was presented with a set of chain armour, a leather under jerkin, arm grieves and leg grieves and belt, along with a sharp-edged broadsword and round shield, On-Gar was suitably attired and was called first gedriht, this meant Ro-Gan's number two in command of the newly formed warband.

Gedriht was the name of those who form the chief's personal bodyguard and in this warband it would consist of twelve from those boys and half-breeds who won their first-round bouts, all of the others would henceforth be called Geoguth.

All of the Gedriht were equipped with helmet and chainmail along with a shield, broadsword and two-and-a-half-meter long spear. The Geoguth had the best of the rest equipment wise, older segmented or leather armour and a bucket helmet or leather cap and there would be armed with a short stabbing sword, a shield and spear.

Later as the ranks swelled some of the warriors might gain a higher status, that of Duguth, or veteran warrior and other additional warrior types like skirmishers who would only wear leather armour and caps, and have daggers, slings or composite bows.

The rest of this evening Ro-Gan would take to get to know his followers made up equally of humans and half-breeds there was food and drink aplenty and even the older orc chiefs would be seen to walk amoungst them, although the new warband were not treated as equals they had certainly earned the respect of their Orsk masters.

During one such interaction Ro-Gan asked one of the Orsk chiefs why they had to dye their skin each morning, to which he was told so that if they did escape the tunnels and run back to the humans then they would be treated as hostiles and probably killed, it was as he had suspected. Ro-Gan quickly moved the conversation along not wanting to dwell on the thoughts of escape and that unhappy conclusion. Ro-Gan wanted to gain the secrets, he wanted answers, nothing much up until now made any sense, this whole underground set up, Orsk were never this intelligent nor were they ever this organised even when magic was strong in the world his hunger for escape would have to be checked for the time being at least, there was a far deeper mystery a foot and it had ensnared the boy completely.

The following day Ro-Gan was putting his warriors through their paces and speaking to them each in turn about what they could expect and what he ultimately expected from them. Later that day while all the warriors were taken to their work duties, Ro-Gan was taken to meet a new Orsk he had not seen before, this Orsk was old and gnarled with many scars to show for his years. War-Lord Poda-Gog.

Huge like a bear and five foot six or seven, but he was fascinating for another reason other than his scars, for he was decorated with much gold unlike any of the other orcs

Ro-Gan had met so far. Gold arm bracelets that went the length of his fore arm, and chains that huge thickly around his neck. At his side was a huge war-hammer discolored by a large amount of dried blood and dirt from many a battle Ro-Gan imagined.

Poda-Gog, wanted to talk about a fourth coming raid and was explaining the night mission Ro-Gan was to take his warband on, it involved attacking a troop of border guards (Human), that were traversing a main road between two towns that Ro-Gan had never heard of before, his brief was to take out the fighters whether they were male or female, capture any children and to take any weapons or armour and of course bring back any other loot. It was imperative that the mission was to take place at night, so timing was everything, and so that the Humans would believe it was an Orsk warband, which Ro-Gan didn't quite understand at the time but excepted, and it was also imperative that if they took any casualties that they were to be brought back also, on no account must the Humans suspect what has happened.

Ro-Gan's curiosity was growing ever more suspicious when he was handed a folded goat skin square which turned out to be a map. Now Ro-Gan had been schooled by monks in a lot of things but never had he heard that Orsk plan anything in this detail or use maps for what was supposed to be an ordinary raid, they had a language but it was not one that be written down as such.

Even more mystery enveloped the inner workings of Ro-Gan's mind, to have sleepless nights over, but for now he was going to have to put his thoughts and emotions to one side and just follow orders. However, it made him even more determined to liberate all the captives and put pay to whatever evil was going on.

Ro-Gan lead his warband of twenty-four, half Human and of half-breeds, out from the depth and safety of the tunnels for the very first time as their leader, and as he emerged from the torch lit interior to the moon lit exterior, he saw that they were at the base of a great mountain range and before them lay a great and vast expanse of undulating, partially frozen tundra.

The night air was bitter and each warrior shivered as they acclimatised to it themselves, Ro-Gan who was wearing his new (well re-claimed new) armour, took the goatskin map from his trouser pocket and studied it for a moment. Some of the warriors who had earned nothing in combat wore only their tunic and trousers and who had rusty old swords and battered small wooden shields, they were truly shivering to the bone and therefore more eager than most to get moving.

The road that they needed to be on was far to the south west and it looked as though it lay across what could have been a border line, perhaps a neighboring realm more than that Ro-Gan did not know, in point of fact he had no idea where he was at all, even if he was still in some part of the Shattered Kingdoms or not. All he did know was that the target were Humans and they were trained in combat to some degree, but he was assured by Poda-Gog that were no match for Ro-Gan's highly trained warriors.

Orsk warbands were expected to run far and to move swiftly so without further ado they were on the move keeping the high mountains to there right as they travelled straight down following a well-used but poorly maintained track. The journey took what was left of the twilight and not once did they spot another soul nor did they see a single dwelling place, nor even a tree, but all along the length of the mountains they saw what could easily have been more concealed tunnel entrances just like the one they had come from, this made Ro-Gan wonder just how many more encampments like his were there.

The border between the two realms was marked by a rather crude set of wooden posts that had dried out and cracked in many places, dead wood just like this whole landscape apart from the wild grass, and a ditch that contained nothing more than a trickle of water under a frozen canopy.

None of the posts, on closer examination looked cut rather they resembled naturally fallen branches or drift wood from the beach that he knew was nearby somewhere in the opposite direction to what they travelled now.

The fence in places looked like there once might have been barbed wire between the posts but not so much remained today but what did was pock marked with clumps of wool so there must have been sheep in this area at one time, or maybe there still was but he couldn't hear or see any at this time.

It was easy to jump the ditch for all but one, one of the half-bloods, called Sugg, he was one of the Geoguth, the ones who were eliminated in the first round of the competition, sadly he was not in the greatest of health and he was wide at the girth and of very limited intelligence, and if anyone was going to, it was he who slipped as he tried to jump and he landed heavily on the far bank were the others were assembled, his left leg sliding into the freezing water. Sugg yelped like a scolded puppy at the shock of the cold water which made all of the others have to stifle laughter, Ro-Gan hissed for quite as he walked forward toward the stricken warrior and bent down to offer his hand.

"We are no longer in an area where we can count on support even at night, so from here on in, we must muffle our weapons and hold our tongues, the target area is still quite a way head, roughly two leagues away and the sun will be rising before we arrive if we drag our feet.

The road marked on the map turned out to be well maintained and although there were no buildings in sight in any direction Ro-Gan observed that this was a main road, perhaps it joined military outposts as it followed the lay of the land that ran parallel to what he thought was the boarder.

They came a little way along the road, Ro-Gan was obviously looking for something but he was well aware of the time as the sky began to lighten in the far east.

The spot Ro-Gan had eventually chosen gave cover to his warband in a ditch that ran either side of the road but this side had a small coppice of trees in which the warriors could hide. As the sun began to climb in the eastern sky the vibration of feet on road were felt by one of the half-breeds who lay with his head to the ground, and he signaled to Ro-Gan before On-Gar ushered everyone to their positions.

From the east the hazy figures emerged walking slowly along the road it could be seen that there were at least three ox-drawn wagons with them and after a few moments it could be counted that there were soldiers, none of whom wore any kind of armour, but each did hold a spear and a small round shield known as a 'buckler'. It was a mistake to ambush the soldiers here because they had the sun at their backs even though it was still very low in the eastern sky, but Ro-Gan would never make this mistake again.

The soldiers were all wearing woolen tunics in various shades of yellow with slightly darker brown trousers, possibly where the dye has run from being out in the pour rain, the lot of a soldier is not a glamorous one Ro-Gan mused to himself, each had feet shod in leather sandals but again it was noted by Ro-Gan that they made a sort of clipping sound on the surface of the road, the sandals he later would discover had flat metal nails driven in to them.

Ro-Gan saw a very solemn and sorry looking bunch of older men and boys who were even younger than he was, and as they came more into view, he determined that their number was twelve, so including the waggoneers their total number eighteen.

As the column drew level with Ro-Gan's hiding place he could clearly see six men out front, three wagons and six men at the rear, and all completely oblivious to what was about to unfold.

On-Gar stood up from his concealed spot and roared

at the top if his voice before hurling his spear into the flank of the lead oxen, of the six men out front three dropped their weapons and shields and threw themselves to the ground in sheer terror, the other three stood transfixed at this mighty warrior baring his (dyed green) chest and launching his spear, which looked a lot longer and thicker than the ones they carried.

There was no time to think, now was the moment the rest of the warband rose and attacked the soldiers, each picking a single target and launching their spears at that target. The lead ox which was struck heavily by the spear bayed in pain and tore forward almost dragging the other ox with it and the front six soldiers were trampled and became entangled with the oxen and by the trailing leather straps, they died a terrible slow death many with mangled and broken bodies and who were defenseless against the long spears now being poke and prodded at them.

The front wagon lurched up as one of the heavy iron-shod wooden wheels ran over one of the soldiers and it tipped on its side eventually as it cleared the stricken bodies and was gently helped over by a couple of the warband. The second wagon was turned by its driver but went straight down into the ditch on the opposite side of the road, causing the wagon to go over on its side and spilling the two soldiers out, one tumbled head first into the ditch wall breaking his neck instantly and the other was pitched forward between the two oxen, he died an agonising death as the two frightened beasts tried in vain to extricate themselves from the ditch and repeatedly trampling over the Human.

The remaining six soldiers ran up alongside the third wagon neither knowing whether to defend it or themselves and they each died from spear and sword wounds. The whole melee lasted no more than a few short seconds but at the time to Ro-Gan it felt a lot longer, four wounded prisoners were brought before him as the rest of the warband set about looting the wagons.

Ro-Gan wanted to know who these men were and where they were from and what was the reason for them being on this road at this time, the first captured man, one of the older looking soldiers refused to utter a single word, he just stared defiantly, and he was put to the sword by one of the half-breed warriors, Ro-Mir, who, when he realised that Ro-Gan was staring straight at him in utter debrief, could only manage to say "My bad," before walking away and hiding amoungst the others.

The second Human saw this barbaric act and began to whimper like a beaten puppy, and when Ro-Gan stepped towards him and began to question him, the Human was hard to silence in the end. Ro-Gan spoke in the language of the Human, who was surprised at first and although the prisoner's speech was heavily accented, Rogan began to picture where he was.

This country was called Lōrnicā, which from the location on his map, the prisoner was able to say that Ro-Gan was from the neighboring country of Obreā, when he said the name he spat at Ro-Gan's feet. On-Gar slapped the back of his head and told him to show some respect, and although On-Gar spoke the Human language, but this dialect was hard for him to follow or to speak himself properly, and so the man understood nothing of why he had been hit.

The last two prisoners were two young boys around Ro-Gan's own age, one was called Brenn and the other, Willem. They had been the two atop the third wagon and although they were so young, they had jumped down into the melee in aid of their comrades and Ro-Gan was impressed by their spirit, his men didn't seem to be too aggressive towards them either had they had not inflicted anything more than wounded pride on any of the warband, and part of the orders stipulated the capture of young prisoners.

The older man was released after questioning as Ro-Gan's orders were to do just so, his master had said that someone needed to tell the other humans that they had been attacked and by orcs. "Fear is the key" was all Poda-Gog would say, over and over again.

The two boys were to be brought back, again, as instructed as Ro-Gan and so many other boys were as future warriors. Both the boys were scared witless at what had happened and probably at this point thought that they would soon be roasted over an open fire and eaten, Ro-Gan saw the fear in their eyes but for now there was nothing he could do to allay those fears and so he did nothing apart from bound and gag them.

The six oxen were released from their harnesses and chased away while the three wagons with had by now been completely looted were pushed into the ditch as close together as they could. All of the dead humans had been piled on top of the middle wagon and then the wagons were set on fire. Everything the warband could possibly carry was stuffed into haversacks.

The journey back to the tunnels in Obrea was a little slower partly because by now the sun was high up in the midday sky and it was punishingly hot with no building or trees or other shady places, added to that all of the contraband that was taken was beginning to weigh them all down and rations were running low since Ro-Gan insisted that the two boys be kept well fed and watered regularly.

Every step forward was a step nearer to home and Ro-Gan's mood lightened somewhat, and he had removed the gags from the two boy's mouths and began to chat to them partly to allay their fears and because the idea would be that they will soon be joining his warband as his follows.

Once Brenn and Willem had got over the shock of this overtly friendly orc, and the fact that they still had not been eaten, they both began to ask questions of Ro-Gan and why they were spared when some many of the others were not. Ro-Gan grumbled that he only been following orders but that this will all begin to make more sense in the future especially if they did as they told and kept close to his side. Two more Humans even added to his warband would make it uneven and already there were murmurings of unrest at the Humans.

On-Gar joined in with the conversation from time-to-time, as he started to pick up some of the more familiar words that Ro-Gan had taught him. For the last five years he had craved everything that Ro-Gan had to teach him, and now he felt confident enough to engage another Human in conversation. On-Gar did not have any prejudices and truth beknown didn't see himself as any different to Ro-Gan, they were both born to a woman and but for the colour of their respective skins they were equals or sorts.

On-Gar wanted to savior every waking moment of this mission, outside with his comrades, free from any watching Orsk masters and second only to Ro-Gan in the chain of command, this was certainly a life style he could start getting used to, he hated being in the tunnels and he hated the fact that he didn't make it into the ranks of the black guard, nothing to do with his fighting prowess, but because he was three inches to short, every Black Guard candidate had to be at least six foot in height, nothing else mattered, they could be as stupid as the day was long so long as they fit the height requirement.

Shortly after the warband had crossed the broken border markers and while Ro-Gan was still deep in conversation with the two boys, Brenn the younger of the two, spoke candidly.

"I know you are not orcs."

On-Gar was the first to re-act, "Of course we are orcs!" He said before raising his hands above the young one and baring his teeth and making his fingers like claws.

Which Brenn did not see but Willem did and it made him laugh.

"We are green are we not?" retorted Ro-Gan.

"Yes, you are green but your eyes are like my own and

your teeth aren't sharp and pointy, and you still haven't eaten us!"

"We haven't eaten you yet!" replied an astonished On-Gar.

"My Grandfather taught me all about Orsk and he described them to me in perfect detail."

"Ah, so you are like an expert Orsk 'knower' are you little one?" asked Ro-Gan, highly amused with the game that they were playing.

Willem turned round to walk backwards so that he could face his cousin Brenn, Ro-Gan and On-Gar, "Who are you actually because my cousin is right, look at your clothes especially where they have got damp from sweat."

Ro-Gan and On-Gar both looked down at the tunics where the chainmail didn't cover the material, and where the sweat had mixed with the dye from their skin, the cloth was stained green. "Neither do you growl like Orsk do when they speak, and I don't mean when your friend there was being silly wiggling his fingers around and sticking out his tongue,"

Ro-Gan spoke directly to the two boys now and he lowered his voice so that nobody other than On-Gar could hear, "The truth is that I was captured years ago just like you both and On-Gar here helped me to survive while I taught him to read and write and all about the outside world. We work for the orcs but to what end we have no idea but we have fought our way to the top and have been given this warband so we intend to follow our orders until we can find out what is really happening, will you two join our warband and help us two to find the answers we seek?"

Both boys looked at each other and without a word spoken nodded in agreement. Brenn, the younger of the cousins said that his father might be able to help, in fact he went on, "If you let us both go then I could ask my father to bring his army to help break you free,"

Ro-Gan smiled at the innocence of youth, not that he

was any older by much, "So, who might your father be that he can call on an army?"

Willem the older boy told Brenn to "Shut up!" before he turned to Ro-Gan and spoke some more, "His father, my uncle is the Chieftan of a village about a league from where you attacked us and those men you killed were some of his soldiers."

"They aren't very good then are they, they didn't even manage to wound one of us!" On-Gar chipped in, looking very smug as he did so.

"He is a very rich man and he could pay mercenaries to hunt you down and rescue us!" said Brenn.

"Yeah, in fact it was only recently that a man came from Råvenniå to offer my uncle mercenaries to fight for him." Willem stated.

Ro-Gan flashed a look of puzzlement at On-Gar, and kept his own council when he wondered if this far north you would need to even have an army. Lōrnicā, Ro-Gan knew from his studies was in the far north of the Shattered Kingdoms and the countries below it were all allies, or at least from what he could recall they were.

"Tell me boys, how often did your army encounter anyone who wanted to fight it?" Ro-Gan asked.

"Never!" shouted Brenn, "Well not in our lifetime, anyway, but now you have perhaps my uncle will buy those mercenaries after all." Suddenly it was Willems turn to be smug.

Ro-Gan became more curiouser by the moment, was this part of a bigger picture, who were these mercenaries? were Ro-Gan and his warband making arms and armour for them? Did the Orsk know about them, was that why they were making the Half-breeds, to even up the odds? Every question brought up more and more questions and no immediate answers and Ro-Gan was becoming increasingly frustrated.

Just before the sun had fallen in the west the warband had reached the gapping tunnel mouth that marked their return to the large cave at the centre of the tunnels they now called home, as the warband filed in down the first corridor and out into the arena many of the Orsk who roamed the upper walkways, gathered and began to cheer and bang the blunt side of their weapons on the walkway railings.

The biggest cheer was saved for when each of the warband soldiers emptied their canvas sacks of all the loot they had recovered and then when the two boys were pushed down onto their knees just behind all of the loot.

"You have done very well Ro-Gan and as well you who are members of his warband!" bellowed the orc, Snag-Roth.

After a moment or two of complete silence, Chief Snag-Roth signaled to his left, it was a sort of circling of his hand ending with his index finger pointing down at the spoils of the raid. Out of one of the tunnels a group of four Orsk waddled to picked through the loot for weapons and shields, they split the things gathered, into two piles, one half of which they then picked up as best they could and then took it and disappeared down the tunnel, they had come from leaving the other pile just as it were.

"Ro-Gan, take these weapons and share them with your warriors, but do not give anything to those two boys, you must now decide who amoungst your warriors will be rewarded with the best equipment and if any who should be left out, that is the way of the orc.

Ro-Gan picked up each weapon and shield in turn and weighted it in his mind and swished a few different swords through the air to test their weight and balance before singling one or other warrior out from his warband and handing the item to them.

The Orsk chief waited until Ro-Gan had finished before summoning yet another four orcs from another tunnel. "Take all of the woolen garment, pelts, furs and other material things and separate them into two piles." Snag-Roth barked.

This was a slow deliberate demonstration of how things would work hence forth until there was nothing left to divide up, Then Ro-Gan asked what he should do with the two captives.

The chief said that they should be taken to the place where all of the settlement's captive women were housed until they could be placed in a settlement as new warriors, either that or their relatives could pay a handsome reward for their safe return, the last bit of his sentence made the old orc laugh and his laughter was joined by many others, as Human coins meant nothing to orcs unless they could be used to melt down and be made into bracelets of rank.

After everything that needed to done was done Snag-Roth called for any other business.

"Forgive me Lord chief but there is but one thing I have withheld from you, and you have just reminded me, for I do not know if it has any value here." Ro-Gan spoke loudly up to the gallery.

"Whatever are you rambling on about?" Asked the chief Orsk.

"Lord chief I collected many small coins, here in this purse, but I do not know if you value them as the humans do?" Ro-Gan said placatingly.

The Orsk chief once more summoned from the tunnel a single Orsk who walked purposefully over to Ro-Gan and took the purse from him, he then tipped the coins on to the floor at Ro-Gan's feet and stood looking at them all, he counted thirty individual pieces; five of which were gold, nine were silver and the rest bronze and copper. The Orsk grunted and then picked up the gold and silver coins but left the others where they had fallen before walking off back down the tunnel he had come from.

"Ro-Gan, sort the bronze coins from the copper ones, and then smelt the bronze down to make individual bracelets for you and your most trusted warriors, one each mind, that will show your rank amongst the others of your kind. The copper which is the least value must be made into bracelets for the other warriors who fought well but did nothing outstanding, and for those who gained nothing this time, well, to you I say, fight harder next time! Now go, I have to report your return to those who sit above me in rank."

Three days had passed before Ro-Gan and On-Gar were summoned to the Orsk chief once more. His cave was first up a set of carved stairs and then turn right towards the balcony above the arena. The cave had been carved into the wall just off the upstairs balcony and it had a rather crude wooden wall and an ill fitted door. The wood was not unlike that which was used for the border posted, bleach, dried out, and pitted with gaps in between so that it offered some privacy but not that much so that you couldn't hear every word that was being spoken inside.

The orc guard who had brought Ro-Gan and On-Gar to the door, stopped, and then knocked four times, and was beckoned inside.

"Ah, good here you are, have the two boys been returned to your care, of course they have, their kinfolk decided the ransom we offered was agreeable but we reneged on the deal but still took the coin."

"Can I ask why, chief?"

"You just did but I do not have to give you an answer, I should have you flogged for insubordination, that's what I should do!"

Ro-Gan said nothing and just stared straight ahead.

"Oh, don't sulk now, there is nothing worse than a sulking Human, in all of my experience they tend to be even more useless than when they are happy, I will say it is all part of a bigger picture, which you and On-Gar are now part of."

This time Ro-Gan half smiled and nodded his head.

"Now, tell me both do you; how does it feel to wear your bracelets of rank?" the Orsk chief enquired.

"Bracelet of rank?" Ro-Gan looked bemused.

The chief cackled as a wry smile broke out across his deeply lined face. "But of course, you have no idea, each warrior wears a bracelet of rank, Gold being the highest, silver the second, bronze the third and copper the lowest, so you see you two are now able to move more freely and have more privileges around our little kingdom under the mountains

# 3 ESCAPE

Ro-Gan was being trusted more and more and allowed to go further and further away from the sanctuary of the tunnels, all be it to find food and fetch it back but he knew he was winning the orcs trust, and it was rewarded one day when Snag-Roth called him to follow him up a second flight of stairs and to another cave off a main corridor, this one though had a fine wooden front and a better fitting door. Snag-Roth knocked but did not wait to be invited in, instead he opened the door for Ro-Gan who saw that it was the Lord Chief's room.

The Lord chief began his conversation by teasing Ro-Gan, saying that if he had the chance he would run away, even after all the Orsk had done for him.

"Where would we go Lord chief what else is there to see beyond what we have seen already?" asked Ro-Gan.

When the Orsk boss replied this time Ro-Gan detected some reticence in his voice.

"We are but a small settlement, the settlement of Nedrakah, Nedrakah is in fact my name, before your success you had not earned the right even to know that, and now you do!"

"Are there more settlements like this Lord chief Nedrakah?"

"I am the master of two more settlements just like this one but I am not allowed to have any more than 100 warriors at my command at any given time, and I also lay claim to one birthing chamber with thirty human birth mothers, who when in child service the needs of the settlement with strong young half-breeds.

Ro-Gan was horrified to hear the last part of the chief's statement but he gave nothing away and he remained on the outside impassive. "Why do we never see the human women lord chief?"

"They are a commodity, we breed with them, they raise the half-breeds until we harvest them, they are not there for our self-gratification, although it is something I know that humans value, never the less, you would see them and take pity on them, I have seen how you fuss over some of your warriors, you are like a mother hen cluck, clucking, Ro-Gan?"

"Yes of course!" replied Ro-Gan barely able to maintain his composure.

"Anyway, go now take On-Gar with you, go and explore just don't wander too far you have another mission tomorrow."

Ro-Gan and On-Gar ventured down one of the tunnels that the Orsk had come from earlier, at the other end were two large Orsk guards, they held a small shield each but a long-shafted spear which bore, just below the bladed edge, two small axe heads, one either side. On seeing the two new comers the guards quickly crossed their weapons in order to stop the advancing pair.

"Halt! Are you two lost or do you both just have a death wish?" said one guard in the language of the Orsk, not expecting either to understand him, his fellow guard just laughed.

Ro-Gan held out his left arm to show his newly acquired bronze bracelet.

Both guards laughed once more and more heartily this time before stamping their feet and clanging their spear tips together.

A voice no less gruff came from behind the two guards and just enough in the darkness so that neither Ro-Gan nor On-Gar could see who spoke, but it was enough to make the two guards leap aside and stand to attention.

"You must be the new pair, the ones who all the fuss is about, and now I can see why!" said the voice as the form of another half-orc came into view. "Snag-Roth's pet, my oh my, such wealth you flaunt it is no wonder these poor guards are in shock."

"We were told that it would be ok for us to explore." Ro-Gan explained.

"So, it is Hu-man, so it is, and you are welcome to meet with my warband." The figure said, completely ignoring On-Gar who in his eyes brought shame on his race by only coming second. The shapeless figure stepped forward into the light of the lit torch above Ro-Gan. "I am Bal-Dok, we met in the arena, remember, and has you can see I have a silver bracelet which makes me your senior!"

Ro-Gan and On-Gar moved freely amoungst Bal-Dok's warband meeting and greeting each man and half-breed in turn, looking at their impressive bracelets and jewel encrusted necklaces, most of the half-breeds just ignored them or spoke curtly in Black speech, some glanced over and then away as if uninterested in the slightest. One or two, however, did ask how many battles had Ro-Gan or On-Gar fought in, and still others asked how many winters they had been here for, a reply was expected as nobody thought for one minute they could be understood, it was as though On-Gar was a Human as well, or had been corrupted and made deaf or mute or both.

The uneasy peace of this part of the cave network was shattered when a blood curdling cry went up from one corner of the settlements large cave followed by a name that was repeatedly being called out in orcish. "Aatu! Aatu! Aatu!"

The humans and half-breeds parted as the short wild looking creature moved through the rank and file, pushing a shoving as it made its way towards Ro-Gan. Bal-Dok had spotted the commotion and swiftly made his way to a spot just between the creature and Ro-Gan.

"Berba-Shin, what is all this noise and especially on the eve of battle, are you not supposed to be on our side?" cried the half-breed chief in mock outrage.

"Aatu where is Aatu?" the creature begged.

Berba-Shin shuffled into view and for the first time Ro-Gan stood face-to-face with an orc shaman and the last surviving orc female, as far as any Orsk could be sure. She was disheveled and her skin although still green was pitted with dirt and dry blood and she smelled like she had slept all her life in a crypt. Atop her head sat a skull headdress slightly to one side as it had slipped forward and entangled in her greasy mop of long straggly white hair, as she choose to speak her words in Ro-Gan's language non but On-Gar and the other humans from Bal-Dok's warband could understand her, even so, none could work out why she repeatedly asked after 'Aatu', which literary just mean noble wolf.

Bal-Dok meant what he had said about the commotion being caused on the eve of battle and especially since he had no idea what the old hag was saying. Bad enough he had to be courteous to this stinking Human but this was beyond the pale. "Go! Now, Berba-Shin we must spend our evening together as brothers for some this will be their last evening, instead of this racket why not bless my fine warriors with the blood of the sacrifices you have made?"

"Stupid half-breed! If I took the time to relieve myself on you all it would be a blessing" With that Berba-Shin scurried away muttering to herself in Ingolandic one minute and then black speech the next and cackling in between, as she disappeared into the deep dark recesses of the tunnels, and after a few moments of complete silence Bal-Dok raised a goblet of ale and shouted praise be to Aarus, the God of war, and a great cheer went up that reverberated around the cavernous space, which rose even louder as everyone present joined in with the name chanting.

On-Gar turned to Ro-Gan and asked in hushed tones if it were better, they go now before the whole ceiling collapses.

"Why did she approach you in such a way Ro-Gan, she certainly singled you out, why? and what did she mean by calling out noble wolf over and over again?"

"On-Gar I swear I have no idea what that was all about, to be honest it spooked me, anyway, yes let's get out of here, did you hear that we will be taking part in a battle tomorrow along with both of Chief Nedrakah's other warbands and yet we have not been told any of this."

On their way back to their own settlement Ro-Gan and On-Gar saw Orsk chief Snag-Roth.

"Chief it is good to see you, but can we talk?" asked Ro-Gan.

"Umm, did you do something you shouldn't have Ro-Gan?"

"No, nothing like that Chief, no, but we did learn that tomorrow we will be involved in a battle, but I know nothing of this and I should be preparing my warriors."

The orc laughed, "You should be yes, but others think that it better that you and your warriors are not prepared!"

Ro-Gan and On-Gar exchanged puzzled glances, "I don't understand Chief?"

"Think about it this way, you are the first Hu-man ever to lead a warband, you showed great skill and courage and have a thoughtful mind, both the other war chiefs are of a higher status and are half-breeds and they have been greatly shamed by you both, in combat and in other area's so, why would they want to give you any time to be prepared?"

"What?! But surely if we fail and the attackers actually win then isn't that worse for us all."

"Some fates are worse than death, we are Orsk and half-breeds, you should be nothing more than a slave, as it is you are not, but what great things lay in store other than to be trampled on by those who hold the reins of power?" Chief Snag-Roth shook his head and fell silent and was still shaking his head as he walked away, "Get some sleep Ro-Gan and you too On-Gar, who knows tomorrow you might find yourself in the afterlife picking crud from between the toes of the gods!" Snag-Roth laughed as he went about his way.

"On-Gar, we need to do something this is stupid, and I for one have no intention of sacrificing my life to make anyone else look good or to pick bits from between the toes of the gods!"

"Was Snag-Roth serious, about the toes of the gods I mean?"

"Don't be so ridicules On-Gar the gods love us and secretly so does Snag-Roth."

"Whatever, Ro-Gan, but we will not win any friends either with the gods or the other warbands."

"We are not here to win friends, but I do take it personally when the lives of my warriors are at stake."

All night Ro-Gan put his charges through their paces, he taught them shield wall tactics just as he remembered from his years with the strange man in his dreams, he had a bad feeling about all of this and he just wanted to get through it with the minimum loss of men and Half-orcs.

Brenn and Willem both wanted to join the fight but Ro-Gan refused their request, they might have had experience in their militia but this battle might be against their own people, Ro-Gan's, no, would very definitely mean, no, this time. However, they were allowed to train late into the night with the warband as they also had knowledge of shield wall and other combat tactics.

The following morning chief Snag-Roth came round

later than usual to rouse the warband.

"Get up you mangey dogs, get up you have a battle to fight!" Snag-Roth bellowed at the weary warriors of Ro-Gan's warband.

"Chief if this was the first, we were to hear about this battle then it is a pile of dung!" Ro-Gan certainly made his feeling known to the chief.

"Did you think I would bring breakfast as well, hmm, I am sorry to disappoint, now get dressed everyone is outside waiting!" Snag-Roth was in a belligerent mood, war was a serious business.

As Ro-Gan and his warriors strode out of the tunnels and into the morning light many found themselves shielding their eyes even though at this time the sun was behind them.

Half-breed, Chief Lug-Ran was the first to catch sight of Ro-Gan's straggling warband.

"Good of you to join us Hu-man I hope you got a good night's sleep and are refreshed and ready for the battle."

"We are good and ready, lead the way lord and master!" was all that Ro-Gan could say, anything else he kept to himself other he thought they wouldn't even make it as far as the battle.

"Do you wish for us to follow your lead or have you made other plans, Lord Chief?"

"We have been informed that a Thegn is coming this way from over the border with Lōrnicā, with his army that at our spotters best guess is at least one hundred strong, they seem to think that we will either give them their money back or honour our agreement to return their two captured children!"

Ro-Gan turned to On-Gar and whispered, "No how on earth do they know that those boys are here, I wonder?"

On-Gar was equally quite in his reply, "This stink's worse than Lug-Ran's arm pits!"

Chief Lug-Ran raised his right arm into the early morning air and shouted, "On wards!"

All three warbands broke into an immediate canter while keeping their respective shapes alongside each other.

Coming with the sun behind them meant that the army of Lōrnicā would be surprised by their sudden appearance but even more so because they might be thinking that orcs can't be outside in the daylight, even so Ro-Gan had a feeling deep down in his gut that that this day was really about some other purpose, but what that was escaped him for the time being.

As the two armies came within a couple of hundred yards of each other they deployed in formation, those from Lōrnicā, resplendent in green dyed woolen tunics with chainmail shirts, five-foot round shields and eight-foot spears. They formed up thirty men wide three rows deep with shields interlocked.

The Three warbands were in an adhoc formation within their three individual formations and without another word, all three warbands were ordered to charge, Chief Lug-Ran gave the command even though he must have known that this attack would be smashed to pieces on the shield wall in front of them.

Some of the humans threw javelins from the rear rank over their own soldiers and they hit with steely precision taking out around fifteen warriors across the front of the charging warband. Some of the warband returned fire by throwing axes and short spears of their own but most hit harmlessly into the shield wall.

When the two groups clashed together the warbands were almost immediately repulsed, fight as hard as they might they just could not break through the Human's front line, Ro-Gan knew it would be a disaster if they fought this way for much longer but he was reluctant to do anything else while Lug-Ran was in command.

On-Gar offered some encouraging words when he said that soon the Humans would tire and then the strength of the warbands would start show, but Ro-Gan was not convinced and so he began to think of a strategy.

After what seemed like hours, but was in fact only minutes, it appeared that Lug-Ran's centre warband was beginning to cave in as more than half his warriors were dead or lay dying in the grass, The Humans saw what was about to happen in the centre of the orcs line and the whole of the third row of their army bunched up behind their own centre as reinforcements, for what looked like a final push to break the Orsk.

Lug-Ran took a blow to his sword arm which went limp and fell uselessly to his side and he only saved himself from certain death by bringing his shield up quickly to hammer his enemy's sword out of the way, but then he took another blow to his exposed left leg and this time he went down on one knee as what was left of his centre warband rallied around him. This was the moment Ro-Gan cried out to his warriors, "Shield wall on me!" and all of his remaining fighters locked their shields and pushed back at the two thin rows of humans Infront of them.

Ro-Gan had drilled his warriors for hours the previous night and that was beginning to pay off now as his flank began to turn the humans in on its self. More of the humans were starting to charge into the middle by now thinking perhaps that they had already won but instead it just added to the weakening of both their left and right flanks. The second warband that fought on the right was equaling beginning to take advantage of the thinning ranks before them but they had already lost their own cohesion and both wings were involved in one mass brawl.

Ro-Gan's warband had by now completely turned the left flank of the humans and was pressing home utilising his unit's fearsome strength, those humans suddenly found themselves fighting not only the withering centre but on their left side as well, and as suddenly as that, the Humans themselves broke in to a writhing mass of bodies fighting on all sides and some even turned and ran from the battle altogether.

By the time the sun was high in the midday sky the battle was over with over seventy humans lying dead or dying, as for the warbands, only a badly wounded Lug-Ran and five of his warriors survived, along with eight more from the other warband belonging to Bal-Dok, and sixteen from Ro-Gan's warband.

On-Gar wanted to chase after the Humans who by now were throwing anything away that would weight down their escape, armour, weapons, shields and helmets littered the route away from the main battle and the Humans were utterly defeated. The rest of the day was taken up with collecting all of the equipment that lay strewn across the battle field and then by savaging for fire wood to make funeral pyres and piling the dead bodies up and setting them alight, any wounded were also thrown unceremoniously into the hungry flames, causing many of those wounded to scream and beg for mercy.

By the night fall the wild animals of the area came to feast on anything that was left, drawn by the smell of the blood-soaked field. Many of the Orsk were then able to come out of the caves and tunnels and take stock of the battle site and it was at this point that many of those present stopped what they were doing as a large white creature came bounding across the field howling and with its fearsome fangs bared. Smoke from the burning pyres mixed with the cold night air and danced and swirled as the oncoming beast glided through the air effortlessly between leaps.

Some of the Orsk and those who survived the battle just dropped everything and turned towards the safety of the distant tunnels and ran, as if the wild creature the size of a small horse was running after them personally.

Ro-Gan saw that the Chief, Lug-Ran, was left unattended and badly wounded his bodyguard, as they also were in full flight, but Ro-Gan's first instinct was to protect a stricken comrade, nothing more, and so he ran towards the chief, On-Gar shouted a warning, "Look out!" When the creature, fangs and claws out, was almost on the fallen half-breed leader.

However, it was Ro-Gan who arrived first and with just a split second to turn his whole body, shield on arm to cover both himself and the left side of Lug-Ran's crumpled body. The white creature smashed into Ro-Gan's shield with such force it shattered the ash and iron construction into several pieces. With his right-hand Ro-Gan dug his spear into the wet sticky earth and such was the force of the creature's lunge that it drove its self-deep on to the bladed weapon, slicing its open from just under its chin right down to it back legs, and then the spear snapped and the creature landed with a thud on top of both Ro-Gan and the badly wounded orc lord.

On-Gar cried in disappear, transfixed by the sight of blood suddenly explode from everywhere and the creature flatten its self on top of both Ro-Gan and Lug-Ran. There was nothing to be seen except a small white island in a sea of scarlet red. Now all those who had ran began to return tentatively back to the rows of dead bodies, they came in utter astonishment at what they had just witnessed, but there was not a one amoungst them who were brave enough to get that close in case the creature was stunned and not dead.

Lord Chief Nedrakah arrived after about half an hour accompanied by the female Orsk, shaman Berba-Shin, she was screaming at the top of her voice, Aatu, Aatu, over and over again, whatever was unfolding was completely incomprehensible to any but herself.

Chief Nedrakah shouted at On-Gar and some of his warriors to pull the creature off the two stricken bodies and they just stood and looked, not even knowing where one body began and another ended. They had to be commanded twice more before they did dare to push their hands into that sea of blood and guts, but as they pulled at the body of the creature, they all recoiled in horror, because there was something stirring deep within the creature's abdomen. Berba-Shin now pushed her way forward once again shouting, "Aatu!"

Without fear or thought for her own safety the wizened old female orc plunged both her arms in deeper than any of the warrior did and she dragged from the creatures inhered a tiny blood-soaked version of the dead creature, and began to yelp, and just as soon as it was pulled free Berba-Shin started to nuzzle it with her face, and no longer shouting but whispering the word "Aatu" over and over again. She didn't seem to care that her face was rubbed red with the hot sticky blood of this small things mother.

Chief Nedrakah again issued the order to pull the creatures body clear of their two fallen warriors, once more, and as On-Gar and several others did so, to everyone's amazement both warriors were alive and began gasping for air.

The following day after everybody had washed down and slept for some hours Ro-Gan, On-Gar and the two other warband chief's, Bal-Dok and Lug-Ran were all called upstairs to a meeting with the orc Warlord Poda-Gog. Already present in the meeting room was the female shaman Berba-Shin, still blood stained and smelling for more fouler than she ever had, and clutching the small creature from the night before, like her life depended on her holding it, but it was no longer red, someone, probably the old Orsk, had washed the blood off its coat, and here it was pure white like the driven snow, and it was treated with such reverence.

The creature had the appeared of a wolf cub, but with one other strikingly distinctive feature, one blue eye and one that was green. Those in the know already guested that it was a white warg welp and Warlord Poda-Gog wanted to keep it as his own personal property, and he reached over to relieve the Shaman of her burden, and she reluctantly allowed it to be taken.

White wargs are a once in a generation anomaly, an Oman of immense power and prestige especially in the Orsk world, and with the edition of eyes that were different colours this minuscule bundle was considered to be token, a familiar from the Gods, the most valuable possession one could ever own, if indeed one could even own a token from the Gods.

Ro-Gan waited until everyone was seated before he began to speak.

"Silence!" bellowed Warlord Poda-Gog, causing the buddle of white fur held tightly on his lap to jump up and yelp.

"You do not have the right to speak at a council of chief's, Hu-man, your rank does not even give you the right to lick my boots, you who have caused our great cause to be set back years!"

Ro-Gan stared silently in disbelief.

"Chief Lug-Ran are you well enough to speak?" asked the Warlord.

"Yes, Lord Poda-Gog, I am stunned in my right arm, and I have a wound on my left leg otherwise I am, I will be perfectly fine?"

"Then you will speak, now, so that we can all see what went wrong yesterday?"

One or two of the other high-ranking Orsk began to bang the table top with fists.

"That coward, Ro-Gan, and his warband hid behind their shields when I shouted to charge the battle plan would have proceeded perfectly if he had just followed that order." Lug-Ran recalled.

"Chief Bal-Dok, is this account exactly has you saw it?"

"Yes, Lord Chief, Chief Lug-Ran and I were executing your plan perfectly until this filthy creature's cowardice."

"Berba-Shin it would seem that not even your intervention can keep this wretched Hu-man alive much longer, what say you Shaman?"

"I say let not I speak, but let the God's speak for us!"

the old hag cackled.

"What are you babbling about foolish women, you are only here because you are the last of the true Orsk shaman, but you have already been out maneuvered."

Just at that moment Berba-Shin burst into the ancient tongue of the Orsk, the black dialect of ancient times, they language of the gods, that should never be spoken in front of any other than the goddess of blood herself.

"Sandraudiga, she who dyes the land red, I implore you to speak to this council today, tell us what we must do!"

Silence befell the room.

For some time only the yapping of the white warg pup was herd until Berba-Shin broke the mood and silence by asking the warlord why he held on to the pup so tightly.

Warlord Poda-Gog let go of the warg, in fact so confident of the pup staying with him he raised both arms above his head and smiled at the orc woman, the pup turned a couple of times on Poda-Gog's lap before it promptly cocked it's leg up and pee'd up Poda-Gog's tunic. Poda-Gog roared at the tiny white bundle, and the creature yelped one more time and then jumped off his lap, and under the table that separated each of the individuals from one another.

The pup went straight to the feet of Ro-Gan and began sniffing his boots it's tiny white tail wagging furiously, then it looked up just once with those piercing eyes and jumped on Ro-Gan's knee.

"The Gods have spoken Lord Chief!" the old wizened Orsk spat the words out daring any to challenge what she had just said.

Lug-Ran clenched the arm of his chair his face twisted in anguish.

Bal-Doc was about to speak when Poda-Gog slammed his fists hard down on the table top, this was not the outcome he had wanted nor could he over turn what appeared to be the will of the God's.

"Leave me, now all of you!" Poda-Gog bellowed.

However, as Ro-Gan held the pup with his right hand to then raise from his seat Poda-Gog held out his hand.

"Stay Ro-Gan we have things still to discuss."

Ro-Gan returned to his seated position and released his hold on the pup, to which the pup stretched up to lick Ro-Gan vigorous about his chin and face.

Poda-Gog saw this display of affection and his heart sank, the Gods had truly spoken and all the warlords plans now hung in the balance.

"What would you have me do next Ro-Gan, or perhaps I should ask your new pet?"

"Lord Chief, I am but your humble servant, I have a warband to tend to and I wish only to await on your new instructions, that is all."

"You are a stupid insubordinate Hu-man who cannot follow orders and whose stupidity will put an end to everything we do here in the Kingdom under the mountain, alas. It is the will of the Gods that you are right and I am wrong, go now to your precious warband and lick your wounds I will deliberate on these matters and give my verdict in the morning, now leave me and take your pet with you, GO!"

The settlement of Nedrakah slept a very uneasy sleep that night although one warband remained largely intact the other two warbands or what was left of them plotted and schemed the death of the usurper, Ro-Gan. For his part in all of this, Ro-Gan was content, but the visions in his mind as he tossed and turned had returned and they became to him like a curse, in the form of hot and cold sweats.

Before the evening ended for Poda-Gog too would find his sleep would not be a peaceful one, because one more visitor was abroad and prowling the upper corridors and passageways, and that night and he let himself in to the chamber of the warlord.

"Who dares to disturb … Centurion Vagun-Gad, what brings you so far down in to the belly of the mountain."

"You have caused us all a great deal of dissatisfaction, Poda-Gog, and I have been sent to gain some assurances that all is not as it seems."

"Perhaps we underestimated our faithful half-breeds and a single human as out witted them?" Poda-Gog was having a personal dig at the Centurion who was himself a half-breed under all his armour.

"Perhaps we have underestimated you Poda-Gog, and we should swap your place with Lug-Ran?"

"Lug-Ran is a fool, his mission was only to scare the men of Lōrnicā, dead men after all do not pay their way."

"We all saw what happened, we watched from the hillside, your Hu-man made a plan of his own and killed all but a few of the men from Lōrnicā, he made the two half-breed leaders look stupid and incompetent, the Hu-mans might think that we are weak and that they don't need to invest in our mercenaries to keep them safe at night."

"They don't need your help Centurion, they have not been convinced by your tricks surely that is what you mean, so you come down here and try to lay all of the blame on me, well go ahead I have lived longer than anyone expected and I am not afraid to embrace my ancestors!"

"The half-breeds who fail their initiation in to the black guard are left with you for a reason, and if that reason is purely to die, surely then their death in combat, is a sacrifice to our God's and a surety that our wider plans will work out, Orsk are a dying breed and you have been for years Poda-Gog, hidden away in your caves not able to come out in the daylight, we are the future of Orsk kind!"

"Never the less, as I said you cannot hope to achieve anything with your precious half-breeds unless we, the true blood Orsk help you!"

"Then rid yourself of all these Hu-man's and the useless half-breeds that would bring us all to ruin and we will start the program anew, in this settlement, do I make myself understood?"

"Yes, Centurion, fully!"

At first light the following morning all of the humans and the half-breeds were assembled in the large cave, along with all the survivors from the other two warbands. The balcony area filled with many of the Orsk chiefs from different settlement for miles around under the mountains.

Chief Snag-Roth was the one who raised his hands for silence and began to speak.

"There is but one rule here in Nedrakah and that one rule is to obey orders, if you cannot obey orders, you will begin to question our purpose, and then everything will fall apart."

Voices were herd agreeing with what was said but those voices came from the balcony and those below in the arena stayed silent.

"Lug-Ran you failed your orders, Guards take of this traitor!"

"Bal-Dok you failed your orders also, your failures must be taken care of, guards!"

Several Orsk guards shuffled forward so they stood in two groups around the half-breed chiefs.

"Kill them both!" roared chief Snag-Roth.

"Ro-Gan you will take charge of all of their surviving warriors you may even take their gold and silver bracelets, but know this Ro-Gan you also failed to obey orders but with hindsight your victory brought unexpected benefits, now the Hu-mans are truly scared of us and they will pay even more for our protection, your insubordination though cannot go unpunished"

The white warg pup began to yelp and the Orsk in the upper balcony began to murmur.

Berba-Shin saw her opportunity and stepped forward to speak, "The Gods have had their payment in blood, and they are grateful, but be careful that they do not want an over payment." Berba-Shin did not want Ro-Gan or his pup to be killed, they had to survive this purge, she had seen his time-line continue and above all else, the will of the God's would not be mocked!

Now it was Warlord Poda-Gog's turn to step forward and speak, barely able to contain his anger he spat out his words with venom, "Enough! Ro-Gan and all of you warriors are henceforth banished from this land and you are to empty the chambers where the captive women stay, go now and clean this place of your stench before I call the Black Guard to do it for you!"

# 4 A NEW BEGINNING

Six four weary men, women and half-breeds snaked their way south-east out of the Orsk settlement of Nedrakah. The last words spoken to Ro-Gan before he left was by his old chief Snag-Roth who told Ro-Gan to head east towards the sea and to follow the coast south from there, Snag-Roth told of an old whaling village that the Orsk used to trade goods with, and so Ro-Gan heeded the advice and off they set taking only a sack each of food and provisions.

The ground that lay ahead was frozen solid, there were no paths or tracks to follow and every foot step was across a land of diverts and hidden holes. Walking during the day was not a worry as the orcs could not follow but at night Ro-Gan knew that if they wished they could easily catch up, orcs can run twice as fast as Humans. So, Ro-Gan wanted to put as much distance between them and his convoy.

The coastal area was every bit as open and exposed as the rest of the country away from the mountains, not a single tree in sight and only the undulating ground and constant driving wind and rain to cover their movements, visibility was very poor and any scent that they left on the wild

grass, which the Orsk would try to follow was blown away
by the wind.

After three weary days of walking Ro-Gan began to ease
up on everyone, he knew they were hungry and exhausted
but more importantly he knew they were not being
pursued, he had sent out spotters' night after night and
they reported nothing. So, on the morning of the fourth
day Ro-Gan let them stop and prepare small cooking fires
and fashion shelters from anything they could find washed
up on the beach.

From this day onwards they stopped each morning at first
light for one hour and cooked food for the day, then they
walked until last light and stopped again for another hour
and hot food, they continued this way until they had
travelled right around the bottom of Obreā and following
the shoreline they came to the mouth of a great tidal river.

After walking west for another three days with the high
mountains to their right and following the tidal river they
came to a much smaller river and what looked like more
border posts, Ro-Gan tried to remember what he had
learned from his teachers, this he thought must be on the
edge of another realm, Fōrren perhaps? If so, they needed
to skirt this area while finding somewhere to cross the
river. The inhabitants of Fōrren were not known for their
hospitality.

It took another two hours of walking before the river was
fordable and so the procession crossed out of Obreā
through the very outer tip of Fōrren and into the deep
dense forest that marked northern most Råvenniå. The
river that marked the northern border with Råvenniå was
wider than the river they had just crossed but now at least
they had wood to cut to make rafts to get everyone across
safely.

Once on the other side they caught sight of smoke,
thick blackish grey smoke, someone was burning wood
about a league to the south of them and they didn't seem
to mind who saw the smoke, this was their chance thought

Ro-Gan, but he did not want whoever it was to be spooked by the sudden appearance of a large group of people, so he decided that they would camp here while a small group went forward to scout out the area around where the smoke was coming from.

The rest of Ro-Gan's people didn't need telling twice and for the first time in days hope rose in their hearts and they quickened their pace to the spot On-Gar had pointed to, to set up camp. The canopy of tree branches was so dense even on the outer edges of the forest that the people soon began to warm up, scouts were also sent out to catch rabbits and other small animals to cook so that they could have their first fresh meat in days.

Ro-Gan set up guards around the makeshift camp and then picked the youngest of the two new comers to his warband, the fourteen-year-old boy called, Brenn, and his faithful if very small pup, Aatu and together they set off in the direction of the bellowing smoke deep in the forest interior.

It would be another day before Ro-Gan reached a clearing in the forest, and it was then that he heard the voices of men, he could get the gist of what they were saying but they were heavily accented in dialect that he was unfamiliar with. For all this was supposed to be a scouting mission Aatu got very excited on first sight of the men and he began playing up once more.

The men were selecting various trees to be chopped down and each was armed with large two-handed axes while others hitched horses to the fallen trunks and dragged them away further through the clearing that they had made, for even here there was no sign of a track.

One of the wood cutters reacted to the yapping pup and he signaled to the rest of the men to be quiet. "Whose be hiding, come out now less you be robbers!"

Ro-Gan, cover blown, stepped out into the clearing and raised his hands, Brenn followed suit, and Aatu danced around Ro-Gan's feet leaping and yapping excitedly.

"Friend! We come in peace." Ro-Gan said, trying to keep his words simple and clear incase of any mis-understanding, there were six strangers each holding the axes and looking directly at him with wide eyed wonder as to who he was, why did he speak funny and more importantly where did he come from?

"State your work and where ye lodge." Asked one of the other men, visibly tightening his grip on his axe. Ro-Gan was unarmed except for a dagger that rested in his belt across his waist.

"My name is Ro-Gan and this is my brother Brenn and this here is my, er, pet dog, we are travelers looking for a new place to settle and we come in peace as you can see from my dog, we are cautious but not trying to conceal ourselves or our intentions."

"Your skin is green and you look like Orsk and smell like pigs in a poke, why is this?"

"Our settlement was raided by Orsk many days from here up north, we covered ourselves to look like Orsk and we have been hiding out from them ever since."

"If you are travelers as you say you are where are the rest of your kind and where are your belongings?

"We set up a camp at the top of the forest and we have left everything we own, there with our kinfolk."

"How do you number?" was asked awkwardly by another the woodcutters.

"If you mean how many we number, it is sixty-four but we are men, women and children."

"How many of you are warriors?" the first man asked.

"About twenty-six, but we are all young and have little or no practice at warcraft."

"So, I ask again what is your trade?"

"Most of us are trained blacksmiths."

"Blacksmiths, you are a village of blacksmiths, who were you making your things for, no body lives beyond our village and that is a league or more south of here?"

Ro-Gan hesitated to say anymore for fear of causing

unnecessary worry.

"Speak! And mind your words before your tale becomes impossible to believe."

Ro-Gan felt his heart sink and he turned to his younger companion with tears in his eyes, "We were all captives of the Orsk and they had us making armour and weapons each day until we escaped."

"You must be from Obreā! The Orsk under the mountain, are they chasing you, have you put us all in danger?"

"We have not seen any signs that they might be following us but we have fought them once and many Orsk were slain, so I am sure that they will not bother us again,"

"Bring all of your people to our village, it is about one nights walk away, you can spend the rest of the day there but then I think it is better that you continue with your journey, do you understand?"

"Yes, and thank you, sir, to help repay your generosity I would ask that you cut down twice as many trees and when my people get here, we will help drag them to your village."

The woodcutter turned to his compatriots and waved his arms about himself, "What are we waiting for, come let us chop wood!"

When the rest of Ro-Gan's people arrived at the camp where the wood cutters had waited it was decided that it would be better if they stayed the night and rested, there were many extra trees that had been felled and Ro-Gan wasn't even sure how they would move them at that point. The woodsmen suggested that each trunk would need at least six people to pull it at walking pace.

Ro-Gan got up early the next morning and went round the small groups of his people and began re-lighting the fires that had gone out in the early hours, breakfast would be an important meal especially since they would be hauling ten large trees down a dirt track to a village some miles away.

Some of the woodsmen had been out in the forest and caught a dozen or so rabbits and found some wild mushrooms and root vegetables so that they could make a stew, so that everyone could fill their bellies ahead of the long pull.

As the camp was starting to pack away the woodsmen began to hook their trees to the horses that they had brought with them and On-Gar was splitting the people in to groups of six fairly evenly balanced individuals. Between them they would move those ten extra trees for the woodsmen that would bring them a lot of extra money to buy much needed supplies for their village.

The journey was not an unpleasant one despite a certain amount of pushing, pulling and groaning. The village was called Hundsnes and it was surrounded by thick forest on every side. However, as the large group now approached it could be seen that the trees had been cut back several hundred feet from a high wooden palisade that also ran around the whole circumference.

Hundsnes was not at all what Ro-Gan or many of his companions thought it would be, yes, every building was made from wood, but most of the houses were off the ground on short thick legs and all were covered in layers of turf. Chieftan Gufi Grettersson was waiting at the open gates which were straddled by two towers that rose higher even than the walls.

"Welcome, welcome, welcome, and thank your people for dragging these extra trunks, you must all be tired out and very hungry." The Chieftan said in a warm and friendly voice.

"Where would you like us to take these trees?" inquired Ro-Gan.

"Oh, just leave them there we have plenty more horses inside the village, I will get men to fetch them and take the wood to the saw mills." Replied the Chieftan.

# 5 A PLACE TO CALL HOME

Ro-Gan was informed that the village of Hundsnes produced all the wooden material for Ingolfsfell, the biggest town in the north of Ravennia, it had over five hundred people living here at this time and although the work was hard it was very rewarding. Once the Chieftan had finished telling Ro-Gan all about his home he began to ask questions about Ro-Gan and his people, where had they come from? Where were they heading to? And what were their hopes for the future?

The Chieftan sat around a large open hearth sipping mead from a wooden tankard along with other men who had introduced as his councilmen, Ro-Gan explained everything and wanted to be open and honest and so left nothing un-said that he thought might be important.

At this point Grettersson asked Ro-Gan if he could make a suggestion that he thought my help the large group as they went forward looking for a place to call home. "Drop the Orsk sounding names, for example change Ro-Gan to Rogan, and get yourselves a last name like mine, I am Grettersson because Gretters was my father's name, in fact everyone in this village is somebodies' son or Daughter so their surname ends in son or Daughter!"

For a few moments everyone was trying to say their own names as one word instead of hyphenating it, it caused a lot of laughter amoungst villagers and Rogan's people, and the good ale and fine food didn't hamper the festive like atmosphere.

The following morning Rogan was up with the house servants as they lit the hearth fires and prepared the bread for the day, Gufi Grettersson was up early as well and the two sat down to share food together. "So, Rogan have you thought of a last name yet?" asked the Chieftan.

"As a matter of fact, no, I haven't!" Rogan replied.

"Then I shall help you, there is no point going one foot outside my village if you only have one name, everybody will be wondering who you are and where you came from, we need to make you one of us, I think."

"I Think we both had too much to drink last night and you still have a sore head, Gufi."

"Hmm, I have got it! You are Rogan Ragisson, on account of you looking like a scarecrow!"

"Gufi!" Rogan blurted out in astonishment.

"No, no, you will see, you are Rogan Ragisson and you are the chief of your own warband, looking for some new place to call home, you truly all look like a band of wandering scarecrows, and look you have even brought your wives and children with you, its perfect and I think I know the perfect place for you to fit right in."

"Why can we not stay here and help you chop wood and protect you from any wandering bandits?" Rogan asked innocently.

"Well, for one there haven't been any wandering anything in these woods for generations, and secondly there is nowhere for you to live, unless you think we should knock down part of our defenses to extend our village."

"I see your point, so where is this perfect place you have in mind?"

"Alright, that's the spirit, so if you leave here by the main gates that road leads straight down into the valley, but after one league, maybe less there is a left turn, that will take you all the way to the coast. There you will find a small village with a lot of empty houses, it is called

Kaldakinn, it is very similar to our village in size but it only has a couple of hundred people living there, the main industry is fishing but it is hard work, especially in the Várgolundur sea, and many of the young folk have turned their backs on the water, instead they flock to the big towns like Ingolfsfell or to Langaholt which is a mining village nearby."

"What about the people of Kaldakinn, do you think they would just open up their arms and welcome us, just like that, no questions asked?"

"No, but if you explain yourselves to their council like you did with me then I think they would welcome you, yes, they are hardy folk and do not suffer fools gladly but they know the truth in their hearts."

"What is that, the truth in their hearts?"

"Their village is dying, the population is aging and even now they don't have the man power to land the minke whales which was their main source of income and if by chance they do, well they have to call out for help to land and process them, all of which costs money and does not bring in any extra, they are half starved and very desperate."

"Many empty houses and not very many people, you say."

"Yes, and they have a church, but a congregation of less than ten, the priest, well I want to call him a priest is as mad as the rest of them, he calls himself 'brother Cuthbald', I think he is a monk, not a priest because when I call him that he always scolds me, any you'll see soon enough!"

"Do we just turn up and offer our help?"

"I will come with you and I will bring half the wood your people helped bring here, as a sort of thank you and you can turn it over to the village as a good will gesture, then use the wood to build and repair. Do you know that they don't have any protection from the outside world, no high walls or defense ditches, and look at all of you, so young and strong and ready to defend the village in a fight, no?"

"They need people to fight, in Kaldakinn, but why?"

"No, no, I just meant that they couldn't defend themselves from a fart, nothing more."

"Are you sure this is a good idea, Gufi?"

"Yes, come we must get ready for the journey, I will introduce you formally when we get there, and Rogan, relax, everything will be just fine! They will love all your young people and welcome you with open arms."

The journey to Kaldakinn took most of the morning but the rain held off and the road was well maintained so all were in good spirits. The road snaked around the outer most edge of the forest and a glance over to the right and it was a breath-taking vista of rolling hills and valleys.

As the long winding procession entered the arch denoting the beginning of the village, they were slowly met by what looked like every resident, some walked along side and many formed a large group to the rear. There was a continuous amount of small talk from all the residents as they wondered who these people were with their old friend Chieftan Grettersson.

The procession came to a halt just in front of the village hall, it was a building similar in size and shape to the one in Hundsnes except where as that was constructed solely from wood this building was constructed with stone, or rather many stones cemented together until about half way up then with a wooden section the rest of the way to the roof.

An older man came out to meet Gufi as the column drew to a halt, he carried a staff and his clothes were once quite elegant, alas, now the sands of time had faded their colours and ruffled their edges.

"Gufi! How good it is to see you my old and dear friend." He whistled through a toothless mouth.

"Renwick Heldur, you, old seadog you, how are things in Kaldakinn?"

"Oh, you know Gufi Grettersson, life has its own rewards, but what brings you here and look at you with so many mouths to feed, are you an army on the march?"

Renwick eyed the new comers with deep suspicion, but before another word was said between them Renwick had to shout above the noise of the gathered crowd for quiet, so that the two chiefs could continue with their conversation.

"These poor and unfortunate, and homeless, wretches are friends of mine who have fallen on hard times and who are looking for somewhere to call home, somewhere where their skills are needed and that they can build into a safe and secure home for everyone, look at them, why they could even contribute to the prosperity of your crumbling village, don't you think?"

"What! Stop speaking these words of enchantment! Are you actually asking me if we can take them in, all of them, have you gone mad in your old age Gufi?"

"Renwick!"

"No, no, no, none of your flannel, the answer is no! and before you utter a single word tell me why are most of the menfolk covered in green dye, and they smell worse than old man Porgies fish factory, and that is saying something!"

"Renwick, let me explain, but not out here, let's go inside and show our guest's your wonderful hospitality."

"Wonderful hospitality indeed, why do you not just come out and say it, free food and drink at my expense!"

Rogan asked Ongar to join him but he turned to the rest of his people and said to camp here in front of the village hall and to make camp fires ready cook food. Brenn asked where they should get the food from and Rogan said to send hunting parties out into the fields as far the edge of the forest and catch whatever they could and share the cooked food with the villagers as they really did look half starved, many with sunken cheeks and dark black rings around their eyes.

Inside the once great hall that was now the village hall, four of the council members or elders of Kaldakinn already sat, Renwick made five and the other seven empty chairs were from members who had passed away and not been replaced. Some of those who saw themselves as prominent members of the village did not wait for an invitation and they also crammed inside the hall, they also wanted to hear Rogan's petition and they wanted to have a say on the outcome.

Rogan took nearly three hours re-telling of all of his people's lives prior to arriving at Hundsnes and he spared no detail. When he had finished, he faced a barrage of questions from every quarter, it was impossible for him to answer until Renwick picked up his staff and banged it heavily on the floor three times. Renwick asked the first question, "So, you escaped the Orsk of Obreā, but won't they follow your trail, a trail that leads right here, and won't they want to exact revenge on not only you but on us for harboring you?"

"No, they won't, the Orsk I believe still hold on to their traditions, so they believe that their Gods had blessed our victory, but that the price was too high for some of them to bear, and as I said these were unusual times, a Human winning this contest I told you about, the fight between Lōrnicā and themselves, they have their own traditions and codes and they dealt with me as they saw fit, I had not broken any of their codes, The other two warband leaders should have at least told me what they had planned even if it were a bad plan that lead to defeat I would have followed it, that is my honour, my code, but they choose another path which lead to their own downfall, that was on them."

"You talked about a new generation of half-breeds and Humans but forgive me if I ask where will they get their women from, might they not just come here to take them, or even follow your tracks to Hundsnes?" asked another councilor.

"If they do, my warband will protect you, but I just don't see why they would recapture women they have already banished as a bad lot." Replied Rogan.

"He has a point, Councilor." Remarked Renwick.

"Let me see, you want to bring so many hungry mouths to my village, and then give you not just our food but many of our houses as well, and what do we get in return, do you even have coin?

"We brought you some wood for repairs, but more than that we can help each other, you could teach us all we need to know to help with your fishing industry and with farming crops, we could make arms and armour along with weapons and I think build defenses so that any attacker might think twice before attempting anything."

"Nobody has attacked this village in a generation or more, last year we sighted a long boat coming up from the south, even that turned back when whoever it was realised that they were attacking an empty village, as for any trade with the outside world, the last time we had traders here from Ingolfsfell was over a year ago, even the Sherriff doesn't bother to collect taxes anymore!"

"Then help us to help you to put Kaldakinn firmly back on the map!"

Suddenly the doors of the hall were swung open and a breathless village came inside excitedly beckoning all to come outside immediately.

As they all filed outside and stood on the steps to the village hall and looked out on a sea of newcomers and villagers all intermingling, the sound of laughing and music and even singing became apparent.

"What is going on here!" Demanded Renwick angrily.

"Look the new comers have caught rabbit, squirrel, deer and birds and they are sharing it all with our people, this is a great day of Kaldakinn, the one true God has answered all of our prayers!"

Rogan signaled to Brenn and Willem to bring some of the food to the council members, and Aatu who had until now been very quiet himself suddenly burst into an impromptu dance around the two boys' legs yapping and yelping, everybody who saw the small white dog burst into spontaneous applause.

"This is the white Warg whelp you told us about Rogan?" asked Renwick.

"Yes, this is Aatu, the one so named by the Orsk shaman." Rogan knelt as he spoke with such affection for his little bundle of joy and held his hands out for the creature to leap up on his leg and begin to vigorously lick his face.

"Well, my fellow council members, I should really call for a vote, however, it would appear we have been out voted already, Welcome to your new home Rogan, now let us all eat I for one am famished!"

The celebrations went on long into the night and everybody ate until they could eat no more and drank until they could neither stand nor sit anymore, and it was late the following day before anyone began to stir from their slumber, most of the village slept outside on the green Infront of the village hall.

Rogan and Ongar began to wake their people and tell them to get themselves ready for the day ahead. At one time the village boasted a population of over five hundred men, women and children now it was nearer half that amount and so many houses lay empty with cold hearths and decaying walls and roofs.

"I think the only fair way to divide these properties up is by order of seniority, so, this is what I want each of you to do, each male, Human or Half-bloods, you have to chose if you want to live on your own or ask one of the females to share with you. You women you have the same choice to make, there will be no ill will if somebody is asked but they refuse, the women who have small children must be provided for by the one who picks them or they must determine to go it alone, do you all understand?"

"Yes, Rogan Ragisson," they all shouted in unison

before bursting out laughing at his new name and perhaps their new found luck.

"Good now who is the next most senior warrior after Ongar and myself?"

One of the half-bloods from Chief Lug-Ran's old unit raised his arm sheepishly.

"I have a silver bracelet, Rogan, so it is I!"

"Do you wish to ask a woman to move in with you?"

"Yes, I do," and he walked over to a women called Brunilda who had one small boy and who looked as though she was pregnant with her second.

Rogan didn't need to ask the women for she squealed with delight and ran into the arms of Gnarga Ingamann,

This continued for most of the morning before everybody was where they wanted to be, but before they went off in search of their new home Rogan told them to meet back here early the following day to make good on his promises to the village, they now called home.

For the women there were several options open to them for work, shield maidens, farmers, work in the fish factory, seamstresses or nursery work. For the men the options were more or less the same except they had to train each day as warriors and they had to help teach those from the village who also wanted to fight, shield wall was a new thing for them, a warband usually meant charging like a pack of wild animals, the fastest and fittest first.

Each third and sixth day of the week everyone who was able helped build the new fortifications around the village, some dug out the ditch while others built up the embankment and yet other chopped and shaped the wood for the palisades.

For the first time in years the villagers were able to take to the seas again and it wasn't long before they had landed their first minke whale, to which the whole village once more turned out to celebrate. On the seventh day of the week those who wanted to attended the only building in Kaldakinn that was completely made from stone, were welcome to do so, it was the church.

Brother Bryn Cuthbald was not from Råvenniå originally and his accent sounded vaguely familiar to Rogan but why he did not know. After that first meeting together brother Cuthbald took Rogan to one side to speak privately to him.

Cuthbald was a tall man standing another inch above Rogan. He had good muscle structure for a man of the cloth which made Rogan wonder if he once was a warrior, his hair was turning white but it still held flecks of black and his short bushy beard was just the same, he wore a full-length off-white rode which matched perfectly his long white hair and trimmed beard. Rogan noticed a sadness in his eyes, or was it regret, he didn't know, but he noticed that this man of God wore only a rope belt around his waist and carried no weapons except perhaps for a small bone handled knife tucked in to his belt.

"Rogan, I am called Brother Cuthbald, and I serve 'the way' which is not like the established church, that is part of the reason why I left the church, our interpretation of the Holy writings is very different, and what they call a priest I simply call a brother."

"And does our sudden appearance here trouble you, brother Cuthbald?"

"I don't know Rogan, I just can't put my finger on it, no, I am sorry, that did not come out quite how it was meant. What troubles me is that I feel we have met before, and yet I left Marçadia almost five years ago, alas, I am old and my mind sometimes plays tricks, but do you know that you have a Marcadian accent, and while it is music to my ears, it has been such a long time?"

"No, I did not know about my accent, and neither do I know where I am from properly, all I know is that I was a foundling and brought up by foster parents and schooled by the church, before I was captured at a young age by the Orsk and taken to live in the Kingdom under the mountains."

"Ah well, don't take any notice of me now, I am sure that I am just being a sentimental old so and so, Rogan, tell me instead about this beautiful creature who never leaves your side, how did you find him, he seems like he is a dog and yet I think he is something else entirely, may I pick him up?"

Aatu was not renowned for letting just anyone pick him up, one or two unsuspecting souls have in fact been barked at or had long white teeth bared at them, but Aatu licked the man of God and nuzzled him this way and that, much to the surprise of both men.

"Are you a man of God, Rogan Ragisson?" brother Cuthbald asked.

"I don't know what to believe, I know I was brought up to be God fearing, I even remember my baptism, the water was freezing cold, but after five years as a prisoner to the Orsk, I just don't know, I did prey every day but I never really thought that I got an answer."

"And yet, here you are, but I thank you for your honesty, this world is not at all how the Almighty intended it to be, we should all be living in peace but as you already know the world is in turmoil, people are to busy plotting and scheming and always looking to make themselves better in the eyes of those around them, and sometimes even at their expense, rather than to just read the good book, it has all the answers."

"Well brother, I have a lot of my own work to do before I can even consider doing the Lord's work, so I don't think I will be of much use right now to either you or him."

"Ro-Gan I am a great believer in God being able to use whomever he wishes to accomplish whatever his heart desires, anyhow if you need me or just want to talk, you know where I am, until then I will bid you good day."

That night Rogan had the most terrible dream and he woke several times during the night in cold sweats, He saw a figure of a very well-dressed man and his wife, random names would be called out in the emptiness of his mind, and faces would fade in and fade out, sometimes he fought with the man and sometimes he saw himself in the arms of the women, everybody around him was dressed in the finest of clothes then came the night of the attack on the church where he was being taught and then he would wake up, Aatu licked his face vigorously and whimpered in

# 6 ONE YEAR ON

Setunis was the nineth month of the year and a time when the sun would set early in the west and the nights were getting colder and darker. However, Setunis became the new month of celebration, the celebration of thanks giving, for the inhabitants of Kaldakinn, for many years the village had been in decline and the population was beginning to age.

Then came Rogan Ragisson, to some he is a genuine savior, to others an opportunity to grow and fatten their purses, and yet to others he was seen as a trouble maker, but one year on from his appearance and the village of Kaldakinn was well and truly back on the map. The village was growing exponentially and traders and visitors firmly set a visit to Kaldakinn as the first place on their journey and no longer a place to be shunned, so much in demand were oil, candle wax, carved bone wear, and seal skins.

Today was the second day of the month of Setunis and preparations being well under way for the first annual festival of Rogan's appearance, although it has to be said at no time did Rogan or any of his people act superior in any way, they just wanted a home and to be happy, settled, and safe, although unbeknown to Rogan the village council had already decided to mark this occasion by announcing Rogan as their new Chieftan.

Rogan was delighted to welcome all the visitors in person and stood with a few of his most trusted warriors by the village gates, one of the first to appear was his dear friend Chief Gufi Grettersson and his entourage from Hundsnes, Rogan demanded that he and his immediate family come stay at the old chieftain's manor house by the village hall, it had been left vacant since the previous Chieftan died, but kept clean and fresh by the ladies of the village who took it in turns even to put fresh flowers and herbs in every day.

Next through the gates were a delegation from Langaholt, the village just below and to the west of Hundsnes, Chief Arn Sigewulfsson had become a dear friend and supplier of much of the stone used to repair and build around Kaldakinn, many traders also came through in between these vaunted friends, however, a few of the older villagers became decidedly uneasy when they caught sight of the Sheriff of Ingolfsfell, Magnus Steinolf and in particular his son Skuld.

The Sheriff would come each year to collect taxes for the King and Queen of Råvenniå, and out stay his welcome, but this was the first time in a few years he had visited, ever since the village fell below five hundred people.

Magnus felt that it was beneath him and sent his son in his stead, as you might expect tax revenues were very low for those years and Skuld never failed to register his disapproval on these matters, two winters back he said that seeing as though they had not been catching any whales he saw no need for them to have the processing factory and so he burnt it to the ground with the old caretaker still inside, of course petitions were made in Ingolfsfell with the Magistrate and the Sheriff but Magnus always seemed to make the trouble go away.

Magnus came by horseback and as Rogan approached

him, he dismounted and walked over to receive Rogan's welcome hand shake.

"You must be the Rogan Ragisson, I have heard so much about."

"And you must be our esteemed Sheriff, Lord Magnus Steinolf!"

"Yes, yes, and I see you must have spent all of last years taxes on throwing this lavish party, tell me it is not just for me, how could you have known that I was coming after all?"

"To be perfectly honest your Lordship if I had known you were in the company of such a beautiful young lady as this, I might even have had garlands put up down both sides of the road."

Rogan teased.

"Quite so, quite so, please, let me introduce my oldest son, Skuld Steinolf and my dear sweet Daughter, Æstrid."

Ignoring Skuld, Rogan went straight over to Æstrid and kissed her on the back of her lace-gloved hand, and he noted that she smelled like the first flowers of spring.

"I trust you have opened up the old manor house for us to stay, Randolf? Inquired the Sheriff.

"Rogan, my name is Rogan, my Lord, and I am afraid I will have to ask you to find space where you can the village is filling up fast!"

"What about the manor, Rolan?" said the Sheriff with a sullen looking face.

"Full of rats, sire!" Rogan replied plainly.

"Big fat dirty rats!" Ongar added with a grin on his face.

"Oh, that won't do, no, not at all, well we had better make our way forward before the only place left is to sleep in the gutter, heaven forbid, good day to you," and off he went with his family, friends and guards in tow.

Æstrid flashed a genuine smile at Rogan as she rode past him, and he dutifully obliged by smiling warmly in return.

Ingrid Hallgerd, the chief of Rogan's bodyguard, suddenly and out of nowhere stamped the bottom part of her spear on his foot! Apart from Rogan who, caught unawares yelped, everyone one else laughed. Aethelric the Bard, another trusted friend, began to sing a little love ditty while strumming his lyre, an oval shaped stringed instrument. Rogan was not amused and made an excuse to return to the village hall leaving those who made fun of him to stay and welcome all the others to the village.

As Rogan walked up towards the village hall Aatu still happily larking around, he noticed that all the horses and carts that the Sheriff and his people had appeared on where now parked up on the village green, the Sheriff's slaves were busying themselves unloading some of the things that he had brought with him.

On opening the hall door Rogan caught the distinct sound of raised voices, and sure enough Renwick, brother Cuthbald, Magnus, Skuld and a stranger, who Rogan missed at the gate were stood around the table arguing.

"Surely, we have not run out of good ale and fine wine, for what else is there to be in disagreement over on the eve of such a celebration?" Rogan spoke in mock apology.

Renwick turned to Rogan and said, incredulously, that the Sheriff had asked to see all of the books from each of the traders registered in Kaldakinn to get a true picture of our wealth in order to set the taxes for the year.

"It's outrageous!" Renwick finished.

"Surely not tonight, Lord Sheriff, why concern yourself with these matters so soon after you have arrived, after all this celebration will go on for the rest of the week, and I am sure that all of the traders will be here for the whole thing, so you can chase these things up later, yes?" said Rogan.

In actuality Rogan had no idea if the Sheriff was trying to push his luck and his authority or if in fact, he could demand to see whatever he liked and so he needed to buy some time while he went next door to speak to his old friend Gufi.

While Rogan made an excuse to leave the great hall, Magnus decided that he and all of his entourage would stay for the duration right here in the great hall, and he began to shoo everyone else outside and start yelling at his slaves to put curtains up to section area's off.

Gufi was a mine of information on exactly what the Sheriff could and could not do, and even offered to go right over there and tell him to his face!

Rogan thanked Gufi and said instead that after the feast this evening they might both approach the Sheriff in a less public place and when he had been fed and watered, Gufi laughed and told Rogan he was a rascal but shrugged his shoulders and said it was he play.

When Rogan finally walked back over to the Great Hall, he was met on the steps by a very crest fallen Renwick, brother Cuthbald and several of the womenfolk. Even Aatu was beginning to pick up on something else not being as it should be.

"What is it now?" Rogan asked nobody in particular.

Renwick and brother Cuthbald began to speak at the same time then they both stopped and said, "After you," before neither spoke at all.

"Renwick you are the Alderman here, what is wrong now?"

"Rogan that thieving bloated self-opinionated worm has only gone and said that his party will stay in the Great Hall!"

"...And that is where these dear people," Rogan turned to the Ladies and servants, "have placed all the food for the celebrations tonight, alright I see, well Renwick, tell me who does the Great Hall belong too?"

"Since the Manor house was constructed for the Chieftan to live in the Sheriff does have the right to stay in the Great Hall while he is here on official business, but he knows he is just throwing his weight about now, and trying to wind us up."

"Renwick go to the gate and fetch my warriors back here, while I go in and see just game our dear Sheriff is playing."

Rogan strode up the stone steps and through the closed Great Hall doors, to his shock the Sheriff had already invited all of his people to sit and eat and drink from the food that had been placed there. Rogan approached the Sheriff with a face like thunder and his son, Skuld and the stranger could see it and both rose from their seats with hand on sword.

"What is the meaning of this?" Rogan was at boiling point. The Sheriff hadn't even bothered to stop eating or rise from his seat, that was a very specific insult to Rogan's standing.

"You, common peace of filth, how dare you address my father in that way!" spat Skuld while still visibly holding the top of his sword." The stranger just smiled, the sort of smile that a predator would smile while its prey sat only a heartbeat away and totally unawares.

The Sheriff had made his point and eventually he stood up and addressed Rogan, "Thank you so much for the feast you have provided, if I knew you were going to go to all this trouble just for me then I must say I am impressed and I think I should like to visit more often,"

"You actually think we are celebrating a visit from a tax collector?"

"Not just a tax collector, but a friend who has friends in the Queens court if you catch my drift?"

"Oh. Well, pardon me my Lord I had no idea it was like that, perhaps it is because we have a King ruling Råvenniå, as well as his Queen."

"Perhaps, anyway if you leave us now and let us all continue eating this fine food, maybe I can forgive you, now, go, Roderick, you are dismissed."

Skuld and some of the other members of the Sheriff's entourage sniggered as they watched Rogan leave his own

Great Hall with his tail between his legs.

Once outside Rogan called his trusted warriors over to him and told them all about what had happened, they were rightly incensed by insult and wanted nothing more than to march into the Hall weapons drawn and to kill every miserable one of them, but Rogan had a plan.

"Renwick, can you and some of my men round up all of the Barleda ponies up and bring them here, enough to replace every horse the Sheriff came on except for the one Æstrid came on, and replace like for like, putting all the horse furniture on the ponies. Barleda ponies were indigenous to this area and were very short in build with short legs, the saddles would look quite ridiculous on them. After that, when everyone is asleep in the great hall, sneak in and steal all their clothes except for Æstrid, now Ingrid, I want you and your shield maidens to put on your finest dresses and bring ale continually to the Sheriff's guards and make sure there is more than enough to drink inside the hall too, now go, everyone as I wish to enjoy what is left of the evening myself."

"Where shall we take the food for the villagers Rogan, there is still much to fetch out from people's homes and there is a lot of meat still on the roasting spits?" inquired Willem.

"Brother Cuthbald, can we relocate to the church?"

"Yes, of course, by all means, we can fetch some tables and set them up out front, inside the church is only for worship, but outside, well, God be praised but I think this will be a night to remember!" said brother Cuthbald.

Everyone played their parts and the rouse went off perfectly and somehow the ale and wine and food tasted that much better and a good time was had by all.

The following morning the whole village was awakened by the sound of raised angry voices and the clattering of men turning things over and kicking them around.

The noise was of course coming from the great hall, and the villagers formed up in a semi-circle outside on the green. Rogan called to his chosen warriors and six stepped forward, "With me and just be careful to follow my lead, I don't want this getting out of hand and I don't want anyone getting hurt."

All seven began to climb the stones steps to the main doors when suddenly they burst open and an indignant Sheriff stood, in his sweat stained nightshirt with his arms outstretched and bellowing at the top of his voice, "where are my clothes?!"

All of the villagers could now see right inside the hall as the double doors opened quite wide, everyone except the Sheriffs Daughter were still in their night attire. The Sheriff was red faced and in the foulest of moods when once more he demanded to know where is clothes were, but this time he was greeted with a mass of laughter from the villagers.

What made things worse was that his son and the stranger were stood just behind the Sheriff in their night shirts and they were trying to buckle their belts on but getting stuck in the many folds of their night shirts' material.

"Guards!" Magnus screamed in a high-pitched tone.

"Fetch me the horses, NOW!"

As innocently as he was able Rogan asked whatever was the matter and why all the shouting?"

At that point Æstrid appeared from behind her father, fully clothed and looking as immaculate as ever. "It would appear that my father and his men have lost their clothes, Lord Rogan."

Ongar jested that some would have preferred it to have been Æstrid, who had lost her cloths, and perhaps all of them while she at it, Rogan just glared at him!

Æstrid's words were like sweetened honey on the tip of his tongue and unbeknown to him his cheeks were flushed red like an apple of a summer's day.

When he turned to the villagers who were laughing so much, they actually looked in pain, he wanted them to stop in case it began to take a strain on Æstrid. "Silence, my good friends, this is a terrible thing that as befallen our guests, please don't think it is funny."

A Statement which caused another round of withering laughter. Moments later around a half dozen sheepish guards appeared still in their night shirts and holding the reins of the ponies with all of the oversized horse furniture on them, and the villagers erupted now, some whooped and others cheered and the morning quickly descended into hysterical chaos.

The sheriff actually tried to sit astride the tiny pony and his feet were planted firmly on the ground either side of the ponies' flanks, by now even Rogan was struggling to contain himself and had to look firmly in the direction of the Sheriff's Daughter to try to keep a straight face.

Æstrid, was having a hard time not to laugh herself and she brushed past her father and whispered, "Thank you" into Rogan's ear.

"You are most welcome my lady," was all he whispered in return.

"Please except my deepest apologies my Lord, but I think the God of mischief, Kuteus has been having his own fun in the night, give my men some time and I am sure that they can find where your clothes and horses have been taken.

"Well, you had better make it quick then because I unlike my daughter, do not find this in the least bit humorous, now I hope you have all of the money for your villagers' taxes, the sooner I get them, the sooner I can leave this God forsaken place!"

Gufi Grettersson stepped forward with a bag full of coins, "Here Lord I had the good graces to advise my Lord Rogan on the King's taxes, one silver coin for each person over the age of twelve, is that not correct my Lord Sheriff?"

"Hmm, of course, I am neither a fool nor a fixer, Scoppi, take the bag off Chief Grettersson!"

So, the stranger had a name after all, he was called Scoppi. Scoppi was a tall slender man who painted his eyes with thick black liner, that certainly gave him a sinister edge, his hair line was receding leaving him with a high forehead, and on his head he had a shock of jet-black hair that was left to grow upwards and was probably only ever ran through with greasy hands or cold water, he looked incapable of humour, even if he were to be tired down and have his feet tickled with a feather.

Once inside the great hall Rogan saw the full extent of the night before and possibly some of the morning, food was strewn everywhere it had looked as if they had been involved in a food fight, plates and tankards lay everywhere too and many were broken, small throwing axes had been left embedded in walls and wall rugs had been torn apart and hug now in tatters. Furniture was not spared either but that was probably done this morning but all the same tables were damaged and chairs smashed and broken in looked as if a battle had taken place.

Rogan made the sheriff wait until after noon had come and gone, and after all of the villagers had returned to their homes to eat their own mid-day meal, nothing more was brought for the Sheriff and his people and they were left to mill around the great hall.

Rogan offered to walk Æstrid over to the church for afternoon worship, not because he had suddenly found his religion, but because he was enthralled by her beauty, and she obviously enjoyed his, or the effect being with him was having on some who looked on, especially Ingrid, whose face was one jealousy.

The sheriff could hardly say no to the event, he was a pious man himself, even though he had heard rumours about brother Cuthbald and his branch of messianism, the man did seem genuine. As they began to walk towards the church, Rogan noticed that when he put his left arm out for Æstrid to take hold of, Scoppi spat on the floor and made a sign across his forehead like that of the pagans who worship many Gods and Goddesses. Scoppi's unhappiness just about made Rogan's day.

# 7 REVENGE

Some weeks later once all the fuss had died down the village of Kaldakinn settled back into what they have been doing best these last twelve months, making trade goods and making an enviable amount of money, Rogan was voted in as the new Chieftan and he was moved from his modest single roomed house and into the manor house and life really was very good.

It happened on the night of the twenty third of Setunis when the sun had set in the western sky some hours before. Nobody knows how or when precisely it happened as the bodies were not found until mid-morning when the first traders came to the villages main gates which still remained closed.

Rogan and Ongar were called together with his trusted warriors and they found all eight of the gate guards dead, each had been taken down but not killed straight away because they had then been mutilated and left to die slowly in their own blood. Rogan knew instantly that this was revenge by the Sheriff for the humiliation he had suffered and it sent out a very powerful message to the whole village, you are not as safe as you thought you were.

Rogan wanted revenge on the Sheriff but Ingrid Hallgerd the Captain of his Shield Maiden's comforted him and said that there were many ways to deal with this matter but none of them must be done in haste. Ongar agreed and said that they should report this incident to the Sheriff so that they are at least seen to be doing things properly, then when they do have a plan, nobody should be able to suspect them and he would pay for this atrocity.

Rogan decided that he would indeed report this matter to the Sheriff in Ingolfsfell and so he told his most trusted warriors, twelve of them altogether, to get themselves ready for the journey to the Ingolfsfell the following morning, but first things first, these dead guards would need to have a proper burial, and so Rogan and Ongar headed over to the Church to meet with brother Cuthbald.

Whilest two men each dug the eight graves Rogan and the elder went over what might be the best course of action when reporting what had happened. Brother Cuthbald warned from the outset that this might be a trap, either on the journey there are once they were in the town,

Ingolfsfell was ten times the size of Kaldakinn, the brother explained and it had a standing army of over a thousand trained soldiers who were barracked not far from the palace.

Rogan couldn't even imagine the size of the place but he knew that he needed to know every scrap of information he could get even to begin to have a proper plan of action.

Cuthbald said that the town would swallow Rogan up but that was a good thing, do not enter in a group but split up and dress down for the occasion, no weapons on show and no armour either, if it must be warn make sure it is well covered by baggy ponchos, shields would have to been hidden in a cart.

So, the plan was for them to travel together most of the way as a caravan of traders returning south with their wares, then on approach to the main gates of the town they would split into couples and the odd number of men would take a wagon and act as a group of traders. Everything was now set all they needed was to wait for sun to rise in seven hours, the journey to Ingolfsfell would take three days and two nights.

Sometime after Rogan and his twelve companions, and Aatu, had left the safety of Kaldakinn, Rogan wondered if they should turn right at the fork in the road and visit his friend Gufi in Hundsnes and maybe even pick up some more men to accompany them, but Rogan felt he needed to be strong and positive, and that meant standing on his own two feet, he was the Chieftan of Kaldakinn now and he needed to set a good example.

He pulled the reins of his horse to the left, decided against the idea, a visit to Ingolfsfell it would be and so instead he busied himself making a fuss of Aatu who had jumped up on to the saddle of his horse and was trying to position it's self so that it didn't slip right back off.

As they approach the junction Rogan did glance longingly to the right, towards Hundsnes However, Ingrid, who was now alongside him pulled gently on her reins and if Rogan hadn't of stayed left their horses would have collided.

The road from here was long and many peaks and troughs, but it was a good road, well made and solid and completely unknown to any of those who travelled it now with Rogan. That first night they set up camp on a flat piece of open ground just off to the right of the road facing south, Rogan allowed a small fire to cook on but told everyone to be alert at least until night fall when they would have to pair up and stand guard.

The following morning just as the sun rose in the eastern sky the group readied themselves once more for the road, muscles ached and men yawned as they were no longer used to sleeping in the open air on hard ground, Ongar remarked that they were getting old to which his women, Halla Greilanda said that perhaps she should start looking for a younger fitter warrior for husband material, to which they all laughed, some smacking Ongar on the arm and telling him he was either already married or very much under the thumb.

At sixteen years of age Halla was an intoxicatingly beautiful woman with long blond hair, where it was not matted with mud, down past her shoulders, and a figure that belied her strength but demonstrated her agility especially in combat, but what Halla had gained in looks she had definitely lost in temperament, she was a wildcat easy to provoke and hard to calm. Ongar loved her dearly as he too was a warrior at heart and even though they were these days inseparable they had no plans to marry or settle down and have children. Every one of their days was lived as though it was their last.

The second night was not as peaceful as the first at some point in the night one of those on guard duty, Olpaz, one of the half-breeds, heard rustling in the bushes about thirty feet from the camp. He made a sound like one of the wild animals of the night and within seconds everyone was awake and poised for anything.

Aatu, ran straight as an arrow towards the sound and within seconds the howling voice of a Human was heard as the white warg seized whoever was lurking there.

"Get your damn dog off me!"

"Walk into the light so that we can see who it is and then I will call him off." Replied Rogan.

"I am Tostig Saeweard, and these two are my companions, Harek Kormak and Sighadd Ketilbiorn, we are journeying to Ingolfsfell and we saw your fire from a distance and hoped to join your group."

"Aatu, heel! Tell me Tostig, where are you from and why do you journey this far without rations?" inquired Rogan.

"We are from a small farmstead out west, called Ghentweald, we go to seek our fortune, life is to boring where we are from, surely you understand, no?" said

Tostig with a half-smile.

"What makes you say that Tostig, we are but humble traders who have banded together to keep safe, like that of which you seek."

"I beg your pardon; I mistook you for warriors but in my defense, you do not have the way of a trader about you and I am certain that if I were to haggle for your goods, I would see your build and agree to whatever terms you wished to sell."

Aethelric the Bard struck up a few cords on his lyre and began to sing a song of friendship by way of de-activating the awkward tension in the air.

"Ah, a travelling minstrel, anyone who can play so beautifully simply cannot have time to train in combat, forgive me all my lords and ladies." Said the silvery tongued Tostig. However, he was soon left looking bemused as the traders started to put on what looked decidedly like chainmail armour and leather jerkins and the each in turn checked the edges of their swords for sharpness.

"I'm guessing Ingolfsfell is a hard market to sell at if traders have to dress this way that is.

After a hearty breakfast it was time to roll up the sheepskin bedding and pack away the cooking equipment and when everything was stowed away Rogan said it was time to set off as they were hoping to arrive early to get a good place at the market, the sun was rising just ahead of them as they were joined in the caravan by the three newcomers.

The company was ambling along at the speed of the horse drawn wagon when out of nowhere a single arrow fizzed through the air and hit Angenwit Stankeld in the chest just to the left of centre, killing him instantly.

"Ambush!" yelled Rogan as everyone dismounted and dove for cover. A few more arrows fizzed by and overhead, this time one found its mark in the horse on the left side of the wagon, wounding it grievously.

"They are both sides of the road." Ongar called out.

"How many?" asked Tostig.

"I can't see anything with the sun in my eyes!" shouted the bard, Aethelric.

Rogan cursed his luck as he had once before been caught with the sun in his eyes, he spat on the ground and said a little something by way of a prayer to whomever might be listening.

Aatu, doing what any headstrong thoughtless individual does best, broke into a charge and veered to the right side of the road where there was a low stone wall, Ingrid, and her shield maidens, Halla, Sigrunn, and Solveig kept low and ran after the white warg. Now all the arrows were concentrated on the warg but he was to fast and to willey and they all missed him and pinged harmlessly off the dry-stone wall. Willem and Brenn saw their chance and they hopped over the low wall near the wagon and followed in the direction of the shield maidens.

"What should we do?" asked Tostig, but before he could get a reply Rogan and the rest of his warriors were angling Left and bolting forwards themselves. Tostig and his two companions opted to stay by the wagon incase anyone should try to run off with it or its valuable cargo.

Whoever the hidden assailants where they were soon overwhelmed in combat and began to fall one after the other until just two were left alive, one either side of the road. Rogan shouted for them to be spared, he wanted information and to get that these two at least had to be kept alive, the rest who had died were soon stripped of anything valuable or useful and their bodies disposed of behind the low stone wall.

The two captives were tied to the two left side wheels on the wagon while four of Rogan's warriors uncoupled the horses to take of the one that had got injured. Two of the others took Angenwit Stankeld's lifeless body and began to dig a shallow grave for him which they would eventually cover with stones from a section of the wall so that wild animals might not get at his body.

Ongar took up questioning the first prisoner, "Who are you and why did you attack us?"

The prisoner looked at Ongar and spat on his boots,

Rogan hit the second prisoner across the face with the wooden end of his axe causing his mouth to bleed proficiently.

Ongar asked the same question again, and the prisoner still refused to speak.

Rogan raised his hand to hit the second prisoner again when the man shouted out to stop.

"Why should I not hit you, your friend is refusing to speak?" said Rogan.

"He is not my friend; I don't even know him!" the prisoner hissed between dribbles of blood.

Ongar asked the question again and the first prisoner laughed.

Rogan backhanded the second prisoner again this time hard enough to dislodge a tooth, and the man screamed in agony, "Stop! Please, stop!"

"I will stop when you start telling me the truth!" Rogan spoke his words slowly and deliberately, and the man said "alright, alright, I will tell you what you want to know!"

Ongar then took a couple of steps towards the second prisoner and asked the original question, but before the other could answer the first man shouted for him to keep his mouth shut.

Rogan whistled just once and Aatu jumped at the first prisoner and bit him right between the legs, and the man screamed and screamed for the creature to be called off, while blood ran both sides of his trousers along with the contents of his bladder.

The second man began to speak so fast now that nobody could understand a word he was saying and Rogan lifted his right leg and stood on the man's groin. "Stop talking so fast or I will introduce you to my pet, you know the one with his teeth embedded in your friend's crotch."

"I'm sorry, I'm sorry, my name is Arnvid and he is Guthorm and we were waiting for a caravan to come down this way ladened with goods to rob. That is the truth, my Lord, I swear!"

Tostig jostled his way forward and told Rogan to look at both their money pouches, up until now the thought had not even crossed his mind. However, when Rogan pulled the pouch from Arnvid he found that it contained many gold coins, Ongar did the same with Guthorm and just the same it was full of gold coins.

Rogan knew that these two worms would sooner die than cross the hand that paid them so handsomely, but in just that fact he had learned so much, this had to be the work of the Sheriff and to prove it he would need these two would be bandits alive. "Bind them both and throw them over a horse each, collect their other horses and hitch one to the wagon and put the injured Horse out of its misery.

Rogan then counted out some of the gold from one pouch and through the remaining amount to Tostig, "Here have this for your troubles." The other bag now slightly bulging at the seams he gave to Ongar, "Here share it out quickly and evenly we must get back on the road. The party forewent stopping again and instead took dried food from their haversacks to eat, it was getting to be midday and the gate guards would be highly suspicious as it was with them turning up so late.

As they drew near to the gates there was still a considerable amount of people entering and leaving, Rogan hung back first so that everyone could put on their ponchos to hide their armour and then until first Arnvid's horse had drawn alongside him and then Guthorm's and he coshed both of them so that their bodies would fall limp once more and they would be unconscious for a time. Tostig and his two companions bade them all fare well and rode off into the town as fast as they could. "Who do you think they really were Rogan?" asked Ongar.

"I have no idea but so long as they are no bother to us, we will forget we ever saw them!"

# 8 INGOLFSFELL

The Guards at the gates to Ingolfsfell called the wagon with the two bodies over the horses to a halt and demanded an explanation which Rogan dutifully gave, "We are late for selling our goods at market on account of these two lowlife scoundrels attacking our caravan this morning,"

"Why did you bring them with you, why not just kill them and leave them at the side of the road?" asked one of the guards.

"Surely not my good man, wouldn't we then be denying the good people of Ingolfsfell a public hanging?" Rogan implored.

"Who doesn't love a good hanging Cuthwig?" said a second guard.

"I suppose you have a point, but let me first check that he isn't dead and that you are not trying to pull a fast one here!" and the first guard then poked his spear gingerly in Arnvid's backside.

"There look it bleeds! so they are still alive, take them to the sheriff's house, Renton, you show them they way, off you go now and enjoy your stay."

Renton left the party once they had reached the

Sheriff's house, not his proper house but the building in which he conducted his business, but even so it was an impressive place, and to one side of it there were stocks and a large barn with iron cages in where prisoners were put.

Ongar unhitched the two prisoners and helped Aethelric, Brenn, Willem, Rogan and himself carry the two unconscious men inside the Sheriff's house. They were met by a man calling himself Sigegar Youngblood, a young man perhaps around the same age as Rogan. "What have they been up to now?" Sigegar asked.

"You know these two, er, drunks, yes?" Rogan improvised.

"Yes of course I do they are two of Skuld's er, acquaintances."

"Skuld Steinolf?" Rogan asked surprised by the frankness of the young man.

"Yes. That's right do you know him, he will be so grateful that you kept these two out of harms way, I am sure he will have a little something for you, you know what I mean?"

"Oh yes, we have met a few weeks ago in fact, and I am sure he will be delighted that we brought his two friends here instead of leaving them by the roadside."

"I am afraid I don't understand, you found them by the roadside, have they been robbed and beaten, they do look like they have,"

"Yes, sadly they have!" said Rogan truthfully.

"Oh dear, and they were only last night bragging about a big score, perhaps they shot their mouths off to the wrong crowd, eh?"

"Most definitely, you are very wise my friend, very wise, now anyway can we leave them here and can you tell us when we might be able to see the Sheriff?"

"Yes, of course put them in the cage next door until the wake up, they may not be in the best of moods, wouldn't want them smashing the place up, and I think the

Sheriff will be back this afternoon."

Later that day Rogan, Aethelric and Aatu returned to the Sheriff's house and saw that Magnus, Skuld and Scoppi were all inside.

"Rogan! It is so good to see you again, did you ever catch the rascals who took our belongings and horses? Inquired Magnus.

"No, we did not but we did catch two bandits, are they still in your lock-up?"

"No, I don't believe they are, why, what did they do, nothing bad I hope?"

"Never mind, Sheriff, I have come to report a crime that was committed at my village a few days ago."

"Oh! Alright then you had better tell me so that I can see how best we can help you."

Rogan felt his angry boil up inside but he knew that he had to keep his cool or this could end very badly for him and all of his warriors. Ongar sensed his friend's disposition and took up the conversation telling in detail what had happened to the eight guards at the village and then about the ambush on the road, on the way here. Skuld sat impassively throughout Ongar's account with nothing but a grin on his face.

"I am sorry to hear this terrible news Rogan, I really am, a trick or jest is one thing but murder is another thing all together, do you think this is a raid by another group, like the Orsk from whom you escaped?"

"No, I don't think this was a raid, nothing was taken, not even the guards' weapons, this looked more like someone trying to send me a message."

"That is as it maybe but I wonder what is the best course of action, should I return to investigate or would we be better served sending a detachment of soldiers back with, they could always stay a while in your village, perhaps this is a matter for the Jarl to sort out?"

"The Jarl?" asked Rogan.

"Jarl Sigfusson, he is… well the Jarl of Ingolfsfell and

so your village is his village, your people his people if you see what I mean."

The day was getting quite warm and humid and Rogan was beginning to wish he no longer had his armour on, it was itchy and uncomfortable and he wanted to find somewhere to change out of his warrior garb and into something cooler and lighter.

The Sheriff must have read Rogan's mind or just noticed that he was fidgety because he suggested that they stop of at the King's head Alehouse for some refreshments before they continued on to see the Jarl. Rogan and his men were very relived even though they tried to hide the fact. Rogan paid for a private room and they all took it in turns to get changed and there belonging where then stowed on the wagon outside in the keep of young Brenn who was deemed to young to drink by Rogan.

The Sheriff and his son along with Scoppi accompanied Rogan and Ongar first into the alehouse and then onto the great palace at the centre of the town, interestingly where each of the guards in turn bowed their heads to Magnus, the Sheriff, as they let them through the many layers of security, without a single word having to be spoken.

Before Rogan and Ongar were allowed into the main hall at the palace, they were asked to leave all of their weapons outside in the care of a young lady with a generous smile and helpful disposition, whom only scowled when Skuld met with her gaze.

Jarl Gudrod Sigfusson was a slight man just above five-six in height and he was deep in conversation with two ladies who for the moment had their backs turned on Rogan and Ongar.

The Jarl suddenly distracted by the appearance of the new group peered from around one of the women, "Ah, look who is here dear ladies, if it isn't the Sheriff himself, come Magnus we were just talking about you!"

The two ladies turned to face the new comers, "Husband! There you are we were just discussing dinner tonight and we were telling Gudrod that he simply must attend and with his handsome son and wife of course."

Æstrid glanced towards Rogan and her face lit up and she nodded a greeting without speaking a word.

"Matilda! Æstrid! What a delightful surprise." Remarked Magnus, while wondering if they had secretly moved to the palace as they were here so often.

The Jarl leaped to his feet clapping his hands together with glee, "Oh, I do love a family reunion, don't you all?" His graces' smile was infectious until his eye's set on Aatu.

"Oh, there is a dog, why is there a dog, I do hope it isn't messy I have just had these floors waxed!"

Matilda shot a disapproving glance towards her smiling daughter, "Thank you my Lord, but it seems my husband is here on official business so I think we had better leave you to it, but don't forget, tonight and bring your son!"

With that the two ladies shuffled off out of the large room but not before Rogan once again caught the whiff of spring from the scent that Æstrid was wearing, she smiled once more but this time only to herself, she loved the attention of the rough and ready muscle-bound warrior, and she loved even more the effect it was having on her dear brother whom she loathed with a passion. If Rogan was any judge of character one short glimpse at Matilda Steinolf, he thought, would take the shine off newly polished silver, she was built like a pack horse and had the demeanor of a pit viper, the very thought sent a shiver down his spine.

Magnus tried to placate having Aatu present by saying that the dog was house trained, before continuing to re-tell the entire story that Rogan had related to him, before he turned to Rogan and then formally introduced Ongar and him to the Jarl.

Jarl Sigfusson was simply delighted to finally meet

Rogan, he said so more than once, while seeming to hold on to Rogan's out stretched hand for far longer than he needed to.

"So, you are the man who is responsible for making Kaldakinn a jewel in the north, welcome to Ingolfsfell, Chieftan Ragisson and Ongar was it? Two real life Barbarians from the frontier!"

Rogan and Ongar stared across at each other for just a moment and were about to address that remark then thought better of it and said nothing.

"Forgive me for just one moment while I call all of my courtesans in, they simply must see you, you're so dashing if not a little well ordinary looking."

For the next five minutes or so all of the Jarls friends and some of his enemies, without his knowledge filed into and then out of the great hall. "Splendid!" the Jarl quipped. Before he was reminded about the white furry thing with teeth and claws, although it was more what could potentially come from its rear quarters that really bothered him.

The Jarl thought it just better to ignore the animal and so there was no mention of Aatu, just a sharp exhaling of breath, every now and again as it caught his eye.

"The news you bring is indeed very troubling is it not Magnus, and I wonder if like you said this is a job for the army rather than you the Sheriff, what do you think about it?

"I suggested to Rogan that we might send a small detachment of soldiers back with him for a while, they would be useless investigating the murders but they might make the people feel a little safer.!

"Why not garrison the village after all it is incredibly important to us here both strategically and financially, what do say Rogan? Would you like to pay for a detachment of soldiers, eh?"

"My lord, I did not come here to ask for help, I have warriors enough to deal with any problems like that which might arise, and I am sure you have had quite enough coin from my village for this year, your grace, and anyway I came here to seek justice for those who are responsible for the deaths of my men."

"Quite so, quite so, and it is technically my village, but I see your point, so you believe that your men were indeed murdered and that it wasn't your old acquaintances come back to haunt you, because I am told that nothing was taken, is that correct?"

"The only thing taken were the lives of eight of my warriors, and for what reason?"

"What reason indeed, may I ask, Rogan, have you had any run ins with anyone lately, somebody you have crossed perhaps and who is seeking revenge?"

Rogan locked eyes with Magnus.

"No, my Lord not that I would imagine would result in so callous an act, so I ask again, if it pleases your lordship, I would ask for the Sheriff to return with me so that he and his men might investigate this matter further."

"Sherriff, what do think, return with Rogan see what you can see and then report back here in say a week?"

Sheriff Magnus Steinolf was a shrewd man and he could sense that Rogan had marked him as the one responsible for the deaths of his men, and he saw how the Chieftan was trying to arrange the situation so that he would go back to the village with Rogan and his men and that might be the last thing he ever did.

"I am afraid I must decline Jarl; I have important business here as you may recall, however I do know just the man to send back in my stead."

"Ah! You have someone in mind to return in your stead, is that satisfactory for you Rogan?"

"I would have preferred to offer my hospitality to the Sherriff but if he is too busy then I understand."

"Excellent, now I to have some pressing business so if you don't mind, I will beg your leave and let you discuss the details as you go, good day to you all, and Magnus I will see you later for dinner."

"With your son my Lord."

"Yes, yes, with my son, and tell your good lady to stop fretting!"

As the party left the throne room, Rogan glanced over to his left to catch a glimpse of who was next in line to speak to the Jarl, and to his great surprise it was the young man he had met on the road here, Tostig Saeweard.

Tostig had seen Rogan and they both nodded at each other and smiled.

Captain Ricsige Brecott was the man chosen by the Sherriff to investigate the murders in Kaldakinn and he was to take with him Sigegar Youngblood as his scribe. the captain was an older man who was formally in the Queens personal bodyguard until recently when he was retired, since then he has been serving with the Sherriff in Ingolfsfell, secretly at the behest of the King.

Rogan observed a man of good character, serious and studious and firm but fare. Rogan thought that he might be able to confide in this man, and that if he were to be this forth coming, this former Captain of the Royal Guard, might just have knowledge that he did not yet possess.

Outside Aethelric had rounded up all of Rogan's warriors who had been collecting provisions for the journey home, some of the warriors were bragging about drinking competitions they had won against the locals while others talked about liaisons with members of the opposite sex, Rogan and Ongar remained pensive for the time being wondering what lay instore for them.

After about half an hour out the captain began to speak, to Rogan, but not so quietly that Ongar couldn't hear. "You don't much care for our esteemed Sherriff do you Rogan?"

"He's a murdering swine and as corrupt as they day is long, Captain, and he has sent you on a fool's errand, he knows it and I know it."

"Why are you so sure, Rogan?"

"Because on our journey here we were ambushed by his men and the two we brought to him were later released without charge, and they were responsible for the death of one of my men in that fight, "What two men do you speak of?"

"Arnvid and Guthorm."

"I hate to be the barer of bad news but both Arnvid and Guthorm are Skuld's men, and I would wager that his father knows little or nothing about who that little urchin is in league with."

"So, you think it could have been Skuld who killed my men at the village?"

"Probably, although Scoppi Hranfast is Magnus's personal bodyguard I have seen him in secret talking with Skuld plenty of times."

"So what?"

"Scoppi is an assassin of great repute, if it is as you say about your guards and the way they died then it is Scoppi who killed them and he could easily have carried that out on his own,"

"Why are you bothering to come with us if you already suspect that is the case?"

"I'm intrigued Rogan, I want to know what is really going on, and I may no longer be in the service of the Queen but I am very much in the pay of the King."

# 9 NEW FRIENDS

The journey back to Kaldakinn was uneventful and Rogan and his warriors were grateful to be home. brother Cuthbald and Alderman Renwick were both waiting by the open gates to welcome everyone home. Rogan introduced brother Cuthbald to Captain Brecott and his assistant Sigegar and then to Renwick. brother Cuthbald was the only one to question why one who rode out has not returned, but he was greeted with silence by all as they trooped past.

Before anything more that day Rogan insisted that everyone took time out to rest and eat, captain Brecott was invited to stay at the manor house with Rogan. While they ate both men talked about their lives up until the day they met and both realised that they had the answers to each other's puzzle.

Captain Brecott was relieved of his service to the Queen when she announced that she had got a completely new body guard made up of the most highly skilled warriors in the Shattered Kingdoms, and all of her previous guards would be relocated to different posts elsewhere in the kingdom. However, before he was posted the King called him to a private meeting with a nun.

Sister Wenyid Tanner had approached the King about the disappearance of possible hundreds of women from just about every town and village in the Kingdom, including from the royal household. Mostly the women were the sort that weren't missed, drunks, petty thieves, prostitutes and the like, but then it became many women at around the same time including servants to both the King and Queen, and it was always women between a certain age, then about five years ago children too began to disappear without any bodies ever being found.

Rogan agreed that these missing people were the ones like himself who ended up with the Orsk in Obreā, but to what end. Ongar had invited himself in and was listening to the conversation before butting in and saying, "that's where I come in!"

Both men beckoned Ongar to the table to eat with them and the captain said, "Please continue."

"The women were taken to produce babies for the Orsk, the Orsk race is dying out and they see us, half-bloods to secure their future, you see they only have one Orsk female in the whole of the Kingdom under the mountain, and she is probably the oldest living thing on earth, so that was never going to cut it, the plan was to impregnate Human women and to supplement the strength of the half-bloods they would take and teach captured boys like you Rogan to fight with them."

"Ongar is correct, but what I could never work out was why, why do they put Half-bloods and Humans together?"

"Yes, indeed, to what end?" said the captain.

"It has to have something to do with the Black Guard!" Ongar said.

"How do you know about the Black Guard, Ongar?" the captain inquired.

"That is the name of the half-bloods who don't get rejected like I did, and who move up to living on the top of the mountain in a great castle. Rogan, who do you think we made all those weapons and armour for?"

"Do you think that your Black Guard are the same as the Queens Black Guard, they are all at least six foot and clad all in black leather from head to toe and they wear plate armour when they are on duty, built like stone golems?"
Silence befell the room.
"The question is, what are we going to do about it?" asked Rogan.
"Or, what can we do about it?" stated captain Brecott.
"The Queen is setting up garrisons of Black Guards in every city, town and now villagers, what do you both think is going on?" Ongar interjected.
"She is getting ready to seize power from her husband!" said the captain.
"Why stop there, why not seize the whole of the Shattered Kingdoms?" Rogan said wistfully.
"Its no secret that Mârcådiå and Råvenniå have been uneasy bed fellows ever since the Queen's brother King Eadweard of Mârcådiå effectively gave her away to marry King Hamund of Råvenniå when she was just fifteen years of age."
"Did you know that Queen Helga and Matilda Steinolf are best friends and that the Queen dotes on Æstrid, the daughter she never had!" Brecott added.
"It is all still tenuous to say the least, and it begs the question where are we going with all of this?" mused Rogan.
"I say we round up all the fighters from here to Langaholt and attack the Orsk and liberate all the captives, including all the Half-bloods, at least then we can stop this vile practice of women and children snatching." Offered Ongar.
Captain Brecott was all in favour of keeping the Royal family out of this as much as they could, fighting on one front would be about as much as they could muster at this time."
"I say we wait, no attacking anyone until we are absolutely sure who is responsible for what, that way we can continue

to build a case against those in charge while at the same time learn who could help us should this all get out of hand." Said Rogan.

"Aye, lad, I think you are right so now we need to widen our inner circle, but who can we trust?" asked the captain.

"We start with my twelve most trusted body guards, and include brother Cuthbald and Renwick of course."

"Eleven, Rogan, remember we are one warrior short." Ongar pointed out.

"Hmm, Ricsige, I would be honoured if you joined my warband, and then I think we should speak with Gufi and Arn, I am sure they will support us and if so then we at least have an army of around three hundred."

"Gufi and Arn?" inquired the captain.

"They are the Chieftains of Hundsnes and Langaholt, and like Rogan I am sure we already have their support in whatever venture we undertake." Remarked Ongar.

Brother Cuthbald was the first outside of Rogan's trusted warriors to talk to and he immediately said that they should send for a church warden from Mårcådiå, called Leofstan Ealdwulf, he was a remarkable warrior of God and was able to sniff out a conspiracy in a pile of freshly washed laundry, also Sister Wenyid Tanner, she had her own set of valuable skills, as well as being adept with the sword.

Brenn and Willem both asked if they should try to contact Brenn's father in Lōrnicā, he could ask the King to raise an army and join them in fighting the Orsk. Rogan said he would bare that in mind, although he wasn't sure if anyone even knew if the two boys were still alive as they would have had no news in the last year or more.

Aethelric wondered if they should actually send a delegation to both neighboring realms, Fōrren and Lōrnicā as it was most likely they to had lost people to this insidious plot.

Ingrid asked if they were any point in including Jarl Sigfusson in on what they were talking about but Ricsige

Brecott rebutted that idea immediately, "He is a lap dog of Matilda Steinolf and therefore of no use what so ever."

"Right here is the plan, Ongar, Ingrid, Halla and the captain will come with me to Ingolfsfell to look for Sister Wenyid, Aethelric you will take Brenn, Willem, Zaryi and Nariako to Lōrnicā, that leaves, Gunnar, Olpaz, Soiveig, Atli and Sigrunn to make their way to Förren."

Sigegar Youngblood was to stay with brother Cuthbald in Kaldakinn and you can travel to Hundsnes and Langaholt to report some of what we have talked about to Gufi and Arn, but being careful how much you divulge.

"Brother Cuthbald how do you propose we get a message to Leofstan Ealdwulf?" Rogan asked.

"I will send a message via ecumenical means, don't worry it will be very discrete."

It was agreed that the four parties would stagger their leaving times so as not to draw unwanted attention and their individual back stories for family and friends was that they were simply going out to investigate new land as the village is rapidly expanding and suitable sites need to be located.

Aethelric and his party slipped away first as they had the longest journey to make to Lōrnicā, and half an hour later it was the turn of Gunnar's party to make their way to Förren, after another half hour Rogan set out for Ingolfsfell. Brother Cuthbald would follow shortly afterwards as he had the shortest journey to make to the two sister villages.

Aethelric the bard was twenty two years old and was chosen to lead the two boys and the two shield maidens as he was a close friend of Rogan and Ongar and well respected by all the other warriors, he was level headed and intelligent and could go by the cover story that they were a group of wandering players, he, obviously played musical instruments and easily recalled songs or flat out made them up on the spot, Brenn and Willem were having to learn how to juggle but because of their constant mistakes it was thought that they could be jesters, Zaryi brilliant at throwing knives and hitting her target precisely and Nariako was a superb shot with a bow, and her trick was to stand a piece of fruit on one of the boys heads and split it in half with an arrow.

By horse and at a canter the journey as far as the turn in the road to Hundsnes took eight hours and they covered a little over eighteen leagues in that time, when they stopped for short brakes Aethelric would search the hedge rows for herbs and mosses to use in medicine, while the others practiced at their new professions as travelling entertainers. By the time they had travelled the six leagues to Langaholt it was around midday and Aethelric decided that it was only polite to enter the village and speak with Chief Arn Sigewulfsson.

Arn listened to the news with guarded enthusiasm, once brother Cuthbald had been and confirmed Aethelric story he would join in with whatever preparations he could without endangering his village and his people.

Aethelric had asked for advice regarding the journey to Lornica and he wanted to know what sort of people they were, Brenn and Willem's help had stretched as far as, "everything will be fine just let us do the talking." Zaryi was from a realm far to the south west called Talamara and Nariako was from even further to the south, across the Dark Water Channel and a land called Ascomanni, so neither of them had any idea of what lay ahead.

Arn said that he would send some of his warband to guide them to an inland river that formed part of western border between Fōrren and Råvenniå, from there they could hire a fishing boat that could take them all the way to the top edge of Fōrren were the river splits in two, the east branch would take them all the way into Lōrnicā.

Arn asked if they would like to rest a while longer as the journey from here to the fishing village of Heeshem, Arn would give them a written letter baring his seal and some coins with which to pay for the hiring of a boat. That much the Chief said was the least that he could do at this time. After a short break Aethelric's party was on the move, and for the next six hours they had an escort of twelve of Arn's household Guard.

A suitable boat was soon hired and after showing Arn's letter and his seal to the fisherman who boat they would travel in he nodded and took some coins and started to prepare for the journey, Aethelric wondered if the man could read the letter but one of the house guards said that it didn't matter as he looked terrified at the sight of him and his warriors.

The fisherman spoke a heavily accented version of Ingolandic with some unusual local touches which made communication nigh on impossible but for one of the house guards who seemed to reel the words off his tongue like a natural.

The old man said that with the wind against the sail you should be prepared to be on the water for about fifteen hours even though the distance is about the same as from here back to Langaholt, he says there is a storm brewing up north and you will run head first into it at Förren point, so be ready to pitch in and do as he say's or you could be sunk, explained the guard.

"Great, so we can't understand a word he is saying but we might have to do everything he says' if we are to survive this journey?"

"Yes, pretty much, good luck to all, we must be on our way back to Arn."

"Good bye and thank you my friends!"

What the fisherman had neglected to mention was that with the wind against them and therefore a useless sail, they would all have to pitch in and row, Brenn and Willem lasted about one hour until they no longer had the strength to row, the fisherman bellowed something to them through the ever-increasing wind and light rain which sounded like rest, they did not need a translated to tell them to up oars and find space in the bottom of the boat to rest. Zaryi and Nariako found the rhythm of the others who were rowing and soon found that they were competing against each, first to out last the boys which they did easily and then to give the other a run for there money. Aethelric missed the odd pull but otherwise like the shield maidens did not want to give up to soon and appear to lose face, the other men gave grudging cheers as the vessel cut through the water with relative ease and gave the wind no chance to push it back,

By the time the boat had reached the mouth of the river where it separated left towards Lōrnicā and straight ahead to a great expanse of water which led to the open sea, Aethelric realised that they were at the crossing point from where they escaped the orcs, "Look boys, look where we are do you recognise this place?" Both shouted against the wind that they did indeed and their hearts lepped because they both shouted that they knew the way home from here.

At that moment a large gust of wind hit the boat and it lurched heavily to the east and the rugged shore line of Forren, the fisherman shouted something incomprehensible and his men began to row hard as he turned the rudder towards the river bank. "Look he is telling us to do something and to be quick about it." Shouted Zaryi. "Raise the main sail I think, look how he gestures towards it."

So, the five helped to haul the main sail up to the top of its mast and as the boat lurched one more time the sail caught the wind and she was off at a handsome rate of knots, but this time down the left fork in the river and towards Lōrnicā. Eventually the boat came to another small fishing village, this time in Lōrnicā, which Brenn called, Ramscliff, probably due to the number of sheep that littered the cliff side just to the east of the beach where the village lay.

Aethelric paid a little more coin to the fisherman and patted him goodbye on his shoulder and the group climbed the sand in search of someone in authority.

# 10 A FOOL'S ERRAND

Gunnar Helgisson and his party had fallen about an hour behind Aethelric's party by the time they had met with Chief Arn and then been escorted to the small fishing village of Heeshem, it did not matter now because they just wanted passage across the river and for that purpose there was a simple pull-rope ferry so no questions needed to be asked and the escort did not need to go all the way to the ferry with them which might have drawn suspicions so soon after the other party had left.

The ferry was a large wide raft roped together with a raised wooden floor to keep the water off the passengers' feet, it was guided across the water by a team of horses either side and two ropes that went through hoops attached to the raft in each of the four corners, a steersman would then work a paddle to make sure that the raft didn't drift to much while being pulled forward across the river. The journey took about an hour and jurying that time Gunnar kept his own company while Atli and Sigrunn acted like two young love birds who couldn't keep their hands off each other and the other two, Solveig and Olpaz who tried to look happy being together but who unintentionally drew attention to themselves by their Icey body language.

Once ashore they were immediately approached by guards from the local garrison in Axley and asked what their business was and how long they were going to be here. The Chief of the guard a white linen tunic with an armour breast plate that was made up of horizontal strips that overlapped each other and he also wore metal arm and leg grieves, his helmet had a rear neck covering on it and each side there were thick metal cheek coverings. The other three guards dressed similar except two of them had chain mail and one had no armour at all, the chief had a short stabbing sword and the other three carried six-foot spears at metal point that must have added another eighteen inches to the spear's length, each carried a large oval shield, white with red stripes emitting from the centre boss.

Gunnar Helgisson introduced himself first and said that he was here on important business of behalf of the King of Råvenniå and that it was imperative that he speak with someone at the court of King Weagstan Godhelm, and to back up his diplomatic mission he produced a letter written by Captain Brecott of the King's Household Guard.

"I am Chief Pàrlan Breac of His Majesties Guard and I can take you to the capital where you can indeed meet with someone from the King's household who can then bring this matter to the King should they see fit. Gunnar thanked the Chief and asked him to lead the way.

The other four companions seemed to be able to walk away freely without any suspicions largely due to the attention Gunnar was now getting. The four were to shadow Gunnar's journey and make sure nothing happened to him but try to remain hidden as much as they could. The journey from the fishing village to the capitol city four leagues or just over two hours on foot, Förren was a fraction of the size of Råvenniå and very sparsely populated.

Once they had reached the capital Gunnar was asked to

wait at the outer gate house which was a spacious round tower build entirely out of stone and housed fifteen guards, some of which were laying in cots, sleeping, perhaps they were not on duty until the night fell Gunnar mused to himself. Outside Olpaz and Solveig followed the chief as much as they could and the other two, Atli and Sigrunn hung around the tower to keep an eye on their leader. While Olpaz and Solveig were trailing the chief, Solveig suddenly announced that it would be better if they split up just in case. Olpaz wondered out loud, "just in case, what?" but Solveig fained that the Chief was already getting away from them and that there was no way Olpaz was getting inside the Royal palace, so she would follow him inside and she was in no mood to take a negative response so Olpaz said he would wait were he was until she came back for him.

Half an hour later Olpaz caught sight of the chief returning with someone who was of high rank indeed, the newcomer wore a white linen tunic under a beautifully crafted leather top which its self-lay on top of finely linked chainmail, dress chainmail as it was far to delicate to wear in battle, then he recognised the man, he stood around five feet five with jet black hair with a receding front hairline and a permanent scowl with deep brown piercing eyes, it was of course, Tostig Saeweard!

Solveig was nowhere to be seen and Olpaz began to panic, the two men had walked confidently by without noticing Olpaz and just as he turned to follow them he caught sight of Solveig and sighed with relief, so much so Olpaz opened his arms wide to hug his female companion, and to his surprise she reciprocated the gesture shortly before she slipped a concealed dagger between his ribs and held him tight, one hand on the dagger and the other over his mouth to stifle any noise he might try to make.

Olpaz slumped to the ground on his bottom with his knees up and Solveig gently placed his bowed head on his knees and Olpaz breathed his last breath before embracing the darkness.

Solveig quickly wiped the blood off the retracted dagger and stepped away from the dead half-breed before continuing to follow Tostig and the chief. Gunnar had not come on that faithful mission to Ingolfsfell and so had never met Tostig.

The market area was full of people and some soldiers and Solveig needed to put some distance between herself and the body so far only four other people knew who she was and one of them she had only met once in Ingolfsfell, two of the others would be somewhere near the watchtower keeping an eye on Gunnar, Gunnar was not the problem he knew nobody here, Atli and Sigrunn did and they seemed to be joined at the hip this trip.

Gunnar sat on a wooden bench on the ground floor of the tower, watching and waiting, the waiting seemed like an eternity in this unfamiliar, the watching, right now was one of the guards' throwing bits of food from his haversack on to the floor and watching as several rats took it in turns to fetch the food and hide in the straw littered floor or under the wooden benches and cots.

Gunnar wondered if it occurred to the soldier to even offer him some of the food instead of wasting it that way, and it was then that Gunnar began to wonder if this was how they treated strangers, or those they perceived as a threat.

The large heavy door to the tower squealed on its hinges as it was pushed open, the waft of fresh air was a change to the foul-smelling room, chief Pàrlan Breac had returned with a young well-dressed man who he introduced as his Royal Highness Prince Tostig Saeweard of Forren.

Gunnar raised himself from his bench and bowed slightly, the two men looked at each other and smiled. "Well at least they teach you manners where ever you are from, Gunnar, is it?"

"Yes, Gunnar Helgisson, and I have important information from Ravennia, from my lord chief Rogan

Ragisson and a signed letter with the seal of the captain of the Royal Household Guard and the seal of the King himself."

"The King of Râvenniå, then this must be pressing business indeed, but this is not the place that we should discuss these matter's perhaps we shall find a quite room at the palace, come Gunnar Helgisson it would appear we have much to discuss, Pàrlan, I can take it from here. Please return to your duties, oh and one other thing Gunnar?"

"Yes, Lord Prince?"

"Did you come alone, it is not important either way I am just curious as to how important this message really is for just one man alone to convey it, you understand, no?"

"I am alone now, I did have companions who watched over me but only as far as making contact, now I don't know, and in any case, they do not have all the information that I have so their role in this matter is over."

"Ah, I see, and a very clever answer that, Gunnar, very clever."

The prince waved his hand and they left alone the two of them and walked towards the Palace, Atli and Sigrunn were craning their necks to see past the people wandering back and forth, to catch a glimpse of Gunnar, but just as the door reopened and out stepped Pàrlan Breac, Solveig caught up with them both, standing with her back to the tower and blocking completely their line of sight as patchy as it was.

"There you are! She announced with genuine surprise.

"Move Solveig we can't see what is happening!" Atli shouted at her.

"Don't worry that guard has brought someone from the Palace, Gunnar will be taken for an audience with the King, our work here is finished we should get back to Kaldakinn."

"Where is Olpaz?"

"I don't know, we split up to get closer to the Palace,

maybe he got inside unseen, I don't know, but no the less he said if we got separated then he would meet us back at the ferry if it were safe to do so."

"So, we are really going to leave Gunnar here on his own, I find that incredible, seriously?"

"Seriously, yes, we are, that or risk being caught as spies and how will that help anyone, come on we should get moving it is already getting late, both of you!" Solveig spoke forcibly.

Gunnar arrived with the Prince at the Palace and was immediately waved through by all the guards they met. Tostig took them to a room off a long straight corridor that stank of polished wood and their foot falls clomped and echoed off the walls, until they reached the room that Tostig had said would be private. "In here, if you please. Now before we get down to business is there anything I can get you, food or a drink perhaps?"

Tostig raised his right arm and clicked his fingers once in the empty room and as if by magic a servant appeared from a door that didn't look like a door until it was open, Gunnar was impressed.

"I haven't eaten all day, and a drink would be most welcome, thank you, Lord Prince."

"Not at all, if what Pàrlan intimated is true then I think you and I are about to become the best of friends."

The servant returned from the concealed room with a platter of hot food whose centre piece was a full roast chicken, and then he returned with a large silver tankard of ale, which as Gunnar took hold of the prince banged with his crystal, jewel encrusted goblet, "Skoll!"

For the next hour or so Gunnar told the story that he had been given to memory by Rogan, and the prince listened intently while continually calling for Gunnar's tankard to be re-filled.

It took another hour or so for Gunnar to pause as he awaited the prince's response. The prince said that he would send for the king's Chamberlin, he would be the person who would know if women and children were going missing in Forren, Although the prince did say there and then that he hadn't heard anything about this sort of thing from any quarter.

Gunnar belched and said, "T'is very fortunate for you Lord Prince, and for the women and children of this realm!" It was evident that Gunnar was drunk by now and right where the prince had wanted him.

Solveig, Atli and Sigrunn had returned to the ferry crossing and it was getting late and there was no sign of Olpaz, "Should we go and look for him?" asked Sigrunn.

"We can't it would look to suspicious if we three strangers suddenly turned around and went back to the capital, no, we need to board the ferry and return to Kaldakinn, perhaps we can stop off on the way back at any of the farms we pass or Hundsnes to see if Olpaz is at any of them waiting for us."

"But that will take days, and what if Rogan returns to Kaldakinn and we are all nowhere to be found?"

"That's as may be but I am willing to take that chance in order to locate Olpaz." Said Solveig.

The following day the prince crossed paths with his father the King of Forren, and the King asked where his son had been all evening, the prince waved away the conversation saying, "Oh you know me Father if there is a gathering to be had then I simply mustn't refuse, it would be impolite."

"Free drink and plenty of wenches I hope!"

"Of course, father, we have our reputations to keep up."

"Nothing I should know about Tostig?"

"No, dear Father, now stop fretting I have a frightful headache!"

The King laughed as he walked away.

Gunnar awoke with a head that felt like it had been trapped in a vice, and as he slowly opened his eyes, he found it hard to comprehend just exactly where he was, it was cold, dark and stank like an open sewer.

"Ah, finally, I thought you were going to sleep all day!"

said the voice from the figure who hung back in the shadows.

"Where am I, who are you?

"Now, the way this works best is if you let me ask the questions and you just stay quite until I need you to speak, how does that sound?"

"Wait, are those bars, am I in some sort of cell?"

"Oh dear, you're not listening." Said the voice and just then from somewhere else in the shadows someone launched the contents of a bucket threw the bars at Gunnar.

The icy water bit at Gunnar's exposed skin, for then he realised that he had been stripped down to his under garments., and he was about to protest when he checked himself.

"That's better, you're a quick learner after all, good, shall we start with your name and where you are from?"

The questioning went on for ages and Gunnar was having trouble keeping conscious enough to answer all the questions.

"Who is taking the women and children?"

"The Orsk!"

"Why are they taking them?"

"To build an army."

"Why do they want to build an army?"

"I don't know."

"Did you come here with any other people?"

"Yes, but they are long gone now I think."

"Was one of your friends a half-breed?"

"Yes! Olpaz, why have you found him, is he hear?"

"We found him alright, left in the market area, dead!"

"Dead! Who killed him, why kill him?

"I rather hoped you could tell me, if he was your friend, or was he following you and you killed him?"

"Why would I kill him, it would make no sense."

"It would, if, you are lying and he was indeed one of these so-called abductors of women and children, if you admit this then perhaps, we can clear this all up and you can go free."

"I have told you the truth, as I told the prince last night the truth, I came here with letter's baring the King's seal, you must believe me, or we could all be in danger."

Yes, yes, yes, so you keep saying, we are in danger from whom though, really?"

"I don't know, from whoever is building an army."

"I think I understand, you want an army from Förren to march out to Obreā and fight these Orsk who are building an army and while we slip out of our country, what will happen, perhaps Rogan will appear with an army of his own and poof, a wide-open country for him to take for himself or for the King whom gave you his Royal seal?"

At that very moment the door to dimly lit corridor was throw open and a torch was poked through into the darkness.

"What on earth is going on down here and why wasn't I informed!" shouted a voice that sounded familiar to Gunnar.

It was the prince, and he strode over to the other voice who had been asking all the questions, and in the glow of the torch Gunnar watched as the prince slapped the interrogator across the face.

"Imbecile! Open the cell door this man is an honored guest!"

"Yes, my lord prince, I am sorry."

The door was opened and Gunnar helped to his feet and brought to the prince.

"Please except my most sincere apologies for this terrible, terrible misunderstanding, but after you disappeared last night, I was out looking for you with half the palace guard but you were nowhere to be found until I overheard two guards talking about a dead body and a foreigner who was being questioned about his death."

Gunnar couldn't remember anything but he knew with every muscle and sinew in his body that he wouldn't have hurt Olpaz let alone killed him.

The prince took Gunnar to the same room that they had been in the previous night and again asked his servant to bring food and perhaps just water to drink. It was hard for Gunnar not to be embarrassed and truly grateful to the prince and his untimely rescue.

"Well while you were out on your little adventure in my city all night, I found out some information about what we talked about, some women and children have been reported as going missing without a body ever turning up, but thankfully for us, nothing on the scale you have been talking about, in fact less than a hundred across the whole country, but whatever the true figure it is too many to go unpunished, so what is it you are proposing we do about it?"

"One proposal would be for each Kingdom to send an army and together we attack the orcs in their underground settlements and freeing any prisoners we find along the way."

"And you believe, or the Kings' man believes that together our combined forces would be enough?"

"What other alternatives do we have, I wonder."

# 10 An Unexpected Journey

Rogan's journey to Ingolfsfell was quite uneventful this time around which was welcome as Rogan had split his trusted warriors into three groups and he was now travelling just three of them, Captain Brecott and Aatu. There was no pretense this time either as everybody who was anybody already knew Captain Ricsige Brecott and, there was even a tale or two springing up around Rogan and his white dog with different coloured eyes, as Aatu was becoming known, which wasn't far from the truth as a warg was a type of wolf and all dogs came originally from wolves, just far more intelligent and savage.

On the way to the Sheriffs house, it was agreed that they would tell him everything they had found out except anything that was either to connect with his family or the queen, the plan had been all along to blame this on the Orsk, entirely, because that was the only way that Rogan could pull everyone together and form a large enough army, the mere whiff of Human involvement and people would start to point fingers at each other and then any pact would fall apart because nobody would be able to trust each other.

The five companions halted their horses outside the Sheriff's house and tied them to one of the two long posts that sat outside the building, there attention was quickly drawn to some muffled noses over at the large barn were prisoners were kept in cages awaiting judgement,

Rogan saw Arnvid and Guthorm teasing each other over something or nothing but when they saw him, they bolted down the side of the long barn and out of sight.

Rogan was about to mount up when Brecott told him to suck it up, they were murdering small fry who could be rounded up later, for now they had bigger fish to land.

Magnus came outside to greet the captain and merely nodded to each of the other in turn and in no particular order, "Back so soon Ricsige, and you have managed to keep your horse I see!"

"Good morrow, Magnus, yes, we are back because we have a problem."

"Oh! And what is that problem, nothing to serious I hope?"

"Orsk!"

"Orsk?" asked the sheriff sounding genuinely taken aback.

"Yes, I discovered that all eight of the men in Kaldakinn were killed by Orsk."

"How do you that for sure?"

"Two look outs were struck with arrows from a composite bow, and the arrow heads were crude and jagged, like the ones orcs would use, then when I inspected the other six, they had, had their throats cut also with a blade that had a rough jagged edge, a sword or dagger would have left a cleaner cut, so it has to be orcs."

"Orsk from Obreā, so they were coming for revenge, do you think?"

"Yes of course, and why not, they had a score to settle with Rogan and his warriors and that is precisely what they did."

"Well, I can't say it wasn't expected it's probably just the timing, over a year later?"

Secretly the Sheriff was skeptical, he wanted it to be just so, but he felt they were not being entirely truthful.

Scoppi appeared out of the shadow of the inside of the doorway, cleaning the dirt from beneath his finger nails with a long-bladed dagger that glinted every time it was twisted towards the early morning sunrise. A long-bladed dagger just exactly like Ricsige had told Rogan that his men had been killed with, when they spoke in confidence back in Kaldakinn.

"Please, all of you come inside, we have things to discuss, am I right in thinking you will want to exact revenge on these killers?"

Rogan looked at Ricsige, not expecting that reply, in fact they had come here to ask for just that reason but they thought they would have a fight on their hands to get the Sheriff to agree to anything.

"We must go straight to the Jarl, I think if we are to track these monsters down then we are going to need a small army, perhaps even ask our neighbors for help, what do you gentlemen think?"

What these gentlemen thought was that the Sheriff must have known their plan all along and was either aiding them now to profit in coin or power, or he had a plan of his own which they were all ensnared in, neither scenario was good because the Sheriff was already one step ahead of them either way.

"Forgive me Sheriff, but the Jarl doesn't seem like a man of action are you sure he will want help us?" asked Rogan, whose mind was going over different scenarios ten to the dozen.

"Of course, he will want to help, your village is his village remember!" the Sheriff said quoting directly what the Jarl had said at their last meeting.

At this meeting the Jarl did not seem himself, he was distracted and pensive but he heard what the captain had to say and then sought council as he always did with the Sheriff before making his judgement.

"Fetch a scribe! We must record everything in writing." And so, they waited until a scribe was brought from an adjoining room.

Captain Brecott I am putting you in charge of this expedition, you will need to send envoys to both Fōrren and to Lōrnicā, they must be persuaded to attack Obreā on three fronts and with a combined army of not less than a thousand warriors, how does that sound?"

"It sounds very generous my lord, and I am sure that a thousand men will bring the required outcome, but I must tell you that we, I, have already taken the liberty of dispatching envoys and even now we are awaiting their return, your grace."

"Impudent or intelligent Sheriff, what do you say?"

"Most intelligent my lord, most intelligent, just the reason why I suggested the captain in the first place, he is sure to bring us victory!"

"Who-rah! Gentlemen, who-rah!"

Rogan, the captain and the Sheriff all bowed and backed away and out of the room.

"Well, that was remarkably easy." Said the captain to nobody in particular.

It was just as the two groups were about to split up, the captain and Rogan to return to Kaldakinn and the Sheriff to his house when a particularly well-dressed individual came running up to captain Brecott. "Edmun Faulkner, is that really you?"

"Oh, yes my lord captain 'tis I, faithful servant of the King, and I have an urgent message that you must drop everything and come with me!"

"Alright, it sounds serious but we will need a little time to prepare our selves for the journey ahead."

"I have coin for which to pay for fresh horses and food, we are to take extra horses and just swap over when the need arises, now please let us make haste."

The Sheriff wasn't expecting any heartfelt goodbyes so he just casually waved and went inside his house. Hidden out of sight was Skuld and Scoppi, who just inched back from the large doorway of the barn, but close enough to hear what was said before Rogan, Ongar, Halla, Ingrid, Aatu and the captain set off on with Edmun Faulkner to see the King.

Østergård, was the name of the capital of Råvenniå and it lay a little over twenty-eight leagues to the south, a journey on horseback that would take eight hours without stops. Which would give the group plenty of time to talk about just what happened with the Sheriff and the Jarl.

"I don't know how but they are on to us, not everything, but enough, it's giving me a real bad feeling." Captain Brecott spoke first to break the awkward silence.

"I don't see how they could, we have not discussed this

plan outside of us and the other eight of my trusted Gedriht." Said Rogan.

"As well as Renwick, the priest and Gufi and even Arn Sigewulfsson." Halla added.

"I hate to be the one to say it then Rogan, but we have a spy in our camp!" replied Ongar.

"A spy or just one of us getting to drunk and not being able to hold our tongues?"

"It amounts to the same, doesn't it?" offered Ingrid.

"We can rule out most of the ones you mentioned Halla because they would actually only just be finding out about the numbers of men we intend to raise, and the Jarl blurted out the exact figures and if you noticed the Sheriff was taken aback, either by his graces loose lips or by the fact that he didn't even know the specific number himself."

"Well, that's that then, Rogan, it has to be one of the twelve, or one of us even."

Silence followed that last comment from Halla.

As they continued on their journey down the Great South Road, a road that was built using fine cut stone blocks, they decided that it had to be someone outside of those who were present, and so began the conversation about every other member of the twelve that weren't here.

Aethelric and Gunnar were both solid friends of all of those present and they were fully committed to returning to the orc settlements and rescuing the prisoners and then stopping the Black Guard breeding program. Brenn and Willem were ruled out because they were still considered young boys without a care in the world and who would have no interest in this level of intrigue. Atli and Sigrunn were so in love that they could barely have time to breath in between all that kissing and canoodling.

"I don't like where this is leading to Rogan, Olpaz is a half-blood who cannot write in any langue so that would rule him out leaving only Solveig, Nariako and Zaryi, all three of my shield maidens, so I hardly call this a definite investigation." Ingrid retorted angrily.

"What if we start at the beginning and see where that takes us?" suggested the captain.

"We know that the Orsk working alone are not capable of thinking up this whole breeding program, so we need to find out who is really the brains behind it." Rogan said.

"We think that it is the Queen of Råvenniå, and she certainly has the coin to back such a venture." Added Ongar.

"But we don't have any solid evidence to take to the King." The captain put in.

"Yet!" said Rogan.

"No, but we do know that the King and Queen are estranged, I can confirm that." Pointed out the captain.

"And we think that she is trying to put together an army?" said Halla.

"And we want to stop what is happening with the Orsk, the kidnapping and rape of all those women!" Ingrid burst out.

Silence again, rape wasn't something any of them wanted to thing about.

I think we should take a break for a while; this looks like a nice place to let the horses eat some forage and we can stretch our legs." The captain said forcefully.

Ingrid was already sobbing as she dismounted and Halla grabbed the reigns of her horse, "Go sit over there Ingrid I will tend to the horses and come sit with you."

Captain Brecott looked down at the ground and shuffled his feet this way and that, Rogan looked over at Ingrid but looked quickly away, and Ongar told him to go speak to her.

Rogan wanted to. He had never seen her this way and didn't know what to do, but Ongar insisted through clenched teeth, "Just go over there and see if she is alright!"

"I'd rather face all the Orsk with a blunt knife!" was all Rogan could muster.

Reluctantly Rogan walked over and stood above Ingrid who was by now sitting down in the long grass verge at the side of the road, Halla was with her batting flying insects away with her right hand, as she saw Rogan walk over, she patted Ingrid on her arm and stood up to be with Ongar.

"Ingrid, I am sorry if something I said has upset you." Rogan crouched Infront of Ingrid and looked into her eyes.

"Something you said! My God Rogan do you not see anything?"

Tears welled in her eyes as others streamed down her cheeks,

"See? What is it that I am meant to see, Ingrid?" Rogan spoke softly now.

"You talk about your trusted twelve and then you start going through a list of all the males and say why you trust them implicitly, even the half-bloods, but oh no, when it comes to the women, they are the ones you don't trust, it has to be one of them who is the traitor!" Ingrid saw no point in speaking quietly now.

"Ingrid it's not like that, I promise."

"You promise, what? What do you promise, that you will rid the world of all the Orsk, then what who will you start on next?

"Ingrid where is all this coming from, I thought that you and I,"

"You thought what, that you could take away all the pain in the world too? Do you realise that every female warrior that follows you, does so because you freed them from being raped everyday by one Orsk after another, they would follow you to the ends of the earth and back, and all you can think of, is that one of us is a spy!" Then Ingrid lurched forward and dropped her head into Rogan's chest and began to sob heavily.

"I had no idea, I am sorry, I don't think you would betray me."

"Why not I am women aren't I?" she gulped her voice

muffled by Rogan's heavy sheepskin coat.

"But we are." Rogan was finding it hard to say what was really on his mind.

"There you go again, what is it that you think WE are, Rogan Ragisson?" Ingrid now began to beat his right upper body lightly with her left hand, out of sheer frustration.

"Ingrid, when all of this is over, I want to believe that I did it for you, for us."

"Rogan what are you babbling about, what is this, us?" She lifted her head slightly, tears still flowing, her mouth only inches from his.

"I, I am trying to say that I love you!"

"Eh?" suddenly the tears stopped and Ingrid was wide eyed.

"Erm!"

"Shut up you fool and kiss me!" she demanded, and they embraced for a long time.

"Well thank goodness that is finally out of the way, I was beginning to wonder if it was ever going to happen."

Halla just swiped her right hand out and hit Ongar on his right forearm.

"Right, good, now we have got that all out of the way should be get moving again, we still have a way to go."

Rogan helped Ingrid up into her saddle and patted her gently on the leg as she wriggled to get herself comfy. "I meant what I said, Ingrid."

Ingrid held on to the saddles pommel and leant down to whisper in to Rogan's ear, "Its Solveig, she is your spy, she hates the Orsk alright but she also hates the half-bloods especially the ones who came with us, they are a constant reminder to all of our pasts,"

"Are you sure, Ingrid?"

"Yes, I am sure, Rogan, but promise me one thing, if we do see her again, please find it in your heart to be kind to her, she has been through so much."

Østergård, was a city built for another age, some said it

was built by giants from across the Várgolundur Sea, every original building was built from stone, with tiled rooves to finish them off, inside there were plaster walls with painted frescos, and where the buildings had fallen into disrepute they had been patched with timber and wattle and daub. Whoever had built these splendid places had taken their skills with them to the grave.

Rogan felt a cold shiver run down his back, he had seen buildings like these before many years ago, and once more he saw the faces of strangers and heard voices that spoke directly to him from the past, but who were they and where are they now, the cut and design of their clothing was different to any that he had seen so far in Råenniå.

"Rogan, Rogan, are you alright?" asked Ingrid.

"I'm fine, just a day dream on a sunny day with a beautiful girl."

"Should I be jealous of this beautiful girl Rogan?"

Rogan just smiled; he was trying to take in his incredible surroundings.

The city had a solid stone wall all around it, the stone or stones were cemented together, fifteen feet thick and around twenty feet high, in places the wall like some of the houses were in distress and had been patched up with different materials just to plug the gaps and wooden walkways and long wooden posts to take the weight off the repairs.

The population of Østergård was over twenty thousand and apart from an unknown number of Black Guard the city could boast an army of four thousand, cavalry, foot soldiers and militia, they were one of the most formidable cities in the Shattered Kingdoms. The city could boast that it had never fallen to a foreign invader in its entire history.

Captain Brecott was recognised were ever he went and people would actually stop and applaud him even though he now wore no military uniform or trappings, but he still dressed as a nobleman of the city. Whatever the people thought of his companions was any bodies guest, but thankfully the streets were filled with the sound barking dogs or neighing horses so seeing the not so little white dog sat astride Rogan's horse with him brought no attention what so ever, which made a change.

Edmun, the King's messenger ushered the group into the palace via a set of narrow back streets and occasionally a tunnel or two, but soon they were immerging from a set of spiral stairs that lead up to a room where there was a roaring open fire and a table set for a king, in fact there was even a king, King Hamund Arnbjorg was sat in his favour red leather chair, one that had a high back and high enough arm rests so that he looked like he was nestled in all the luxury the palace could offer.

The King stood up and clicked his heels together on the arrival of his guests before bowing to each in turn and offering his hand for them to kiss, the King in turn took hold of Ingrid's hand and kissed it, then he did the same to Halla, Aatu just got another stern look.

The guests were told to sit and eat before any other business was to be discussed, the meals just kept coming and Rogan for one was finding himself continually thanking the servants but turning them away. After about an hour the King began to speak, first by asking about the journey, and then about the situation as far as they knew, and he said candidly that if his wife was involved in any way that she was not above the law.

"So, you think my wife is hiring these half-Orsk as mercenaries, she has about five hundred here alone and many more scattered about the kingdom, mostly in the cities and towns, not so much the villages, but why, not to mention it must be costing her an absolute fortune?"

"We believe that she is planning to seize the throne for herself, and then after that perhaps to march on other sovereign states, who knows, but these Black Guard are not being paid just to stand on guard all day, are they?" stated the captain.

"However, it is not illegal just to hire guards to have them stand around and do nothing at all!" put in the King. "So, what evidence do we have that my dearly beloved has even broken so much as a finger nail?"

"We do have a witness to something else that has occurred in the palace, all be it over a couple of years ago now but it might be the missing link between one thing and another."

"Captain Brecott, I asked for frankness now who is this witness and are they credible?"

If we could just speak with Sister Wenyid Tanner I think we might have our first piece of the puzzle."

"Did you that our dear sister is being put forward for sainthood, and she is still alive, have you ever heard anything like it before, but she will be at the cathedral will she not?"

"That I wouldn't know your excellency."

"Edmun, finish your drink and go find out, it is late in the afternoon now and I don't want our dear sainted sister brought here in her night attire, go, shoo!"

It was another hour before Edmun returned with Sister Wenyid. She was not at what Rogan or Ongar had expected, they might have imagined a rather older plumper women, more matronly type, perhaps, whose voice was gruff and stern, but to everyone surprise Sister Wenyid was lithe and wearing chainmail with a sword at her side, her hair was long and golden and her face was a picture of warmth and compassion.

Rogan was intrigued, "Forgive me my lady, but is it true that you are called a saint?"

Wenyid threw her head back and laughed, "Don't believe everything you hear, I am but a pious sister married to the lord."

"Then he is a very lucky lord, sister!" Rogan said, drawing a hard stare from Ingrid.

"Come now sweet sister tell these noble gentlemen what you have really been up to, after all they have inquired after your credentials."

"Let me tell the story, please sister," implored the captain,

"You boys, honestly, go on then if you must but I had better get a sizeable donation to the church roof fund, if you are to bore me to death!"

Captain Brecott told how three years ago a fleet of Gnomes from Holsettia sailed across the Dark Water Channel, the mighty river as wide as a continent, and landed in a country far to the south called, Faleacia and within weeks that mighty army of savages had swept across the country killing, looting. Raping and pillaging as they went, and no man nor army could stop them.

Sister Wenyid at the time was visiting one of their churches and it was attacked but she valiantly took up the sword of one of the fallen warriors and charged right into the marauding Gnome warband and single handedly killed them all.

"That's not true Ricsige and you know it, I killed but a handful and then the town militia found their second wind and they did most of the killing!" After that Sister Wenyid…and her militia friends chased the horrible little creatures right back to their boats and they sailed away with their tails between their legs.

"Wow!" was all Rogan could muster.

Ingrid bowed her head in Wenyid's direction acknowledging her bravery and spirit.

"Now, if you have all finished with your over embellished stories, can I ask why I was summoned your majesty?"

"I need these gentlemen to hear your story of the confession of Æstrid Steinolf."

"Queen Helga dots on the girl, Æstrid, and when she was thirteen years old to mark the occasion the Queen through a fancy-dress ball and hundreds of guests were invited, young Æstrid was newly a woman after her first bleed, and she was quite the beauty back then, well as the night wore on and people started to leave it was thought time for Æstrid to take to her bed chamber, here in this palace.

Now it was just a short while later that we all heard what was a blood curdling scream, and everyone ran upstairs to the sound that came from the girl's bed chamber, but only her mother, the Queen and myself were allowed inside, there was no one else there at that time. Æstrid, said that she had been attacked by someone, someone she knew, when we asked who that someone was her mother and the Queen were asked to leave the room, she wanted to make her confession before God and to me.

Although the person that forced himself up on her was wearing one of those costumes and a mask, he let slip that the reason he was going to take her virginity was to teach her a lesson, he mentioned something that only her brother, Skuld could have known, not enough evidence to get him convicted by any magistrate at the time, and she was absolved publicly of any blame though she was worse for wear herself with fine wine, and I found out later from the church that the Queen had paid a small fortune to buy witnesses to give Skuld an alibi.

"And now for the second damning piece of evidence, Sister."

"Well, this is harder to prove as the young servant girl who witnessed it has long since disappeared herself, fell off the face of the earth. Anyway, she was going about her duty in the Queens bed chambers when she heard what she thought was laughter and squealing and other matrimonial noises coming from the Queens bedroom, knowing that the King was away on business elsewhere she peered in through the crack in the door, and to her horror there was the Queen in convulsions with Skuld, and both were naked as the day they were born, he being only fifteen himself at the time."

"This is almost too incredible to believe, and your highness I am so sorry that this account has been brought back to mind, shall we stop now and talk some more another time? Asked Rogan.

"No, please let our blessed sister continue, there is more."

"The next time the servant girl caught them together she overheard the Skuld talking about if he were king, he would deliver all of the Queens enemies into her hands, and she quipped, what if everyone in the Shattered Kingdoms were her enemy, what then, and Skuld boldly declared then he would build an army and take the Shattered Kingdoms and give them for a foot stool to her feet."

"You say this girl disappeared, but did she have a name, maybe we can track her down, we have men in three different Kingdoms as we speak."

"Solveig, she was twelve years old at the time I think."

"Solveig Arnulfrid? Wait a minute, she must be about fifteen or sixteen, yes?" Rogan asked Ongar.

"Yes, I suppose, I don't really know."

"How do you know the girls last name, have you seen her, or perhaps you met while captive to the orcs?" inquired sister Wenyid.

"She is one of my most trusted companions, my Gedriht."

"Then we can speak to her in person, your Majesty you see this is the missing piece of the puzzle!" the captain said excitedly.

Just at that moment the double doors burst open and, in the door way, illuminated by numerous torches in the corridor behind her stood Queen, and as her shadow flickered with the torch light the shadows accentuated her features and her standing, she looked both magnificent and terrifying at the same time.

"Oh, my darling Husband you are not having a party without inviting me, are you?"

# ABOUT THE AUTHOR

Shane Kind was born and raised in the north of England and spent many years travelling around the country before finally settling in Cambridge, UK.

Printed in Great Britain
by Amazon

66893738R00078